the book please leave me a review

Thanks

Jill Griffin

Driven to Kill

JILL GRIFFIN

First produced in Great Britain by TN Traynor Publishing

ISBN: 9798343396607

Contents

Dedication

This is for Rob, my greatest fan. —JG

~~~

Acknowledgements

A heartfelt thank you to Tracy Traynor, my publisher, and to David Wake, Helen Blenkinsop, Dawn Bolton, and Rob Griffin for their invaluable feedback as beta readers. Your help, ideas, and unwavering support have been deeply appreciated.
~~~

Chapter 1

Lucy—Present Day

A SHIVER RAN down my back, a familiar shadow that never quite left me. I wondered which ghost had run over my grave.

For 1:30 in the morning, Manchester Airport was busier than I expected. The arrivals hall bustled with weary travellers, all sporting the same bleary eyes and clutching duty-free bags. The baggage handlers must have been on a go-slow tonight.

Doodles filled the page of my puzzle book, as we sat in baggage reclaim, restless and waiting. The belt had been still for what felt like an eternity, the airport's noise pressing in, every minute stretching more than the last.

It had been over half an hour since we landed, and at least twenty minutes since we strolled through Passport Control. *What's the holdup?*

Nodding at each one, I counted at least ten security guards and three armed police officers loitering near the exit. They always say you can never find a copper when you need one—well, tonight, they were out in force. Some people made awkward small talk with strangers; others stared at the clock on the white-washed walls or remained glued to their phones.

Tension was building. Tempers frayed. Voices rose, and the sharp cries of babies and restless children cut through the air.

I nudged Joe. "These kids should be in bed. What kind of parent brings them home on a flight this late?"

He winced, rubbing his ribs. "That hurt. You've given me a bruise."

"Oh, don't be such a baby." But an embarrassed-blush heated my cheeks.

Mum shook her head at me. "Darling, you don't know your own strength."

Dad chuckled. "Stop embarrassing her, Nancy. Look, she's turning scarlet."

Joe grimaced. "Night flights are cheaper. That's why there are so many children." He lifted his t-shirt to show a faint mark on his ribs. "See what you've done?"

I reached for his hand. "Sorry…"

But he slipped his hand into his pocket, ignoring me. Cold shoulder. *Fair enough, I deserved it.*

At long last, the conveyor belt rumbled to life, and our leopard-print suitcases were the first to appear.

"Bit of luck, Joe. Be a love and grab our bags. I'll wait for Mum and Dad's cases with them because Dad's back is still hurting. We'll catch you at the exit."

"Sure." From the way he answered me, I knew he wasn't thrilled.

Strength and confidence oozed off Joe as he headed over to the conveyor belt, I couldn't take my eyes off him. *How did I get so lucky?* He had one of those faces that made people stop and stare—handsome, with Viking-blond hair and a body that turned heads. It made me grin to watch a few women study him as he hauled our bags off the carousel.

He blew me a kiss as he headed toward the exit. I blushed with pleasure, hiding my face behind my book for a moment. My happy-go-lucky, jean-loving man still made my heart skip.

Then I saw it… armed police surrounding him. Ice slid down my back, every muscle in my body tightened. People walking by slowed down to catch a glimpse of what was going on, their curiosity heightening my distress.

Panic rose from my chest to my throat. The urge to run to him gripped me, but I was stuck waiting for Mum and Dad's suitcases, silently willing them to appear faster.

At the point of exploding, I spotted them and yanked them off the belt. A desperate glance at my parents, and we hurried over to Joe, a flood of adrenaline shooting through me.

As we neared the room they had taken him to, my legs weakened and I thought they'd give way. The open door revealed two policemen talking to Joe. Coming to a stop in front of a third by the door, I clutched the case handle to make sure I remained upright. "What's going on? Why have the police stopped my husband?"

One of the officers in the room turned to me. "Who are you, miss?"

"I'm his wife. What's this all about?"

"Mrs Browne, can you confirm you packed your own suitcase?" The officer's flat tone did nothing for my nerves.

Panic shut down my mind. It was hard to think straight. "Yes, but what's that got to do with anything?"

"We have some questions for your husband."

"But we've got a taxi waiting." To make a point, I glanced at my watch. "What's the hold-up?"

"Can you confirm which suitcase is yours?" He pointed at the leopard-print bags.

"Our clothes are in both. Can I speak to my husband, please?"

Handcuffed, with his hands behind his back, Joe's eyes met mine, wide and frightened as I went into the room. Tears prickled behind my eyes and I thought my awful flight meal might be about to make a second appearance. "What's happening?"

The officer checked his watch. "You can have two minutes."

Joe leaned in, his voice low. "Lucy, this is all some horrible mistake. They've stopped me on suspicion of distributing child pornography."

My blood ran cold and I stumbled back a couple of steps. "What?"

"Love, I swear it's a mix-up. They're taking me to Wythenshawe Police Station. I'll be cautioned, and then I'll come home. Go on without me, okay? They've taken my laptop and phone, so I might not be able to call you right away."

I shook my head in disbelief. *This has to be a dream, a horrid, horrid dream.* "But Joe—why? Why you?"

"I've done nothing wrong, I promise you. Just… wait for me. This is a nightmare. I'll explain everything later."

Two officers stepped behind Joe. One gripped his elbow. "Time to go, Mr Browne."

Shoving my hands deep into my jacket pockets, I turned my face away as Joe was led out of the airport, flanked by several armed policemen. My mind refused to process what had just happened and I couldn't watch.

"Show's over," I grunted to no one in particular but glared at the people openly staring.

A deep, creeping unease settled in my gut as we hurried out of the airport. After everything I'd been through—after clawing my way out of the darkness and finally reaching a place of fragile happiness—it felt like I'd walked straight into a war zone. My new life, the peace I had built, was crumbling before my eyes and going up in smoke.

Chapter 2

Lucy—Six Years Earlier

GROWING UP WITH adoring parents, I had a childhood most would envy. I was their 'everything,' and they made sure I knew it. The only thing I ever longed for but never got was a sibling—someone to play with, to share secrets with, to be my friend. As a young child, I endlessly asked for a baby brother or sister. Every time I brought it up, Mum's face flushed a deep red as she stared at the floor, avoiding Dad's wistful glances. His face would crumble, his rich brown eyes dimming, and he'd start pacing the room, a silent frustration settling over him.

The tension would hang in the air until I couldn't take it anymore, and I'd rush to him, planting a kiss on his cheek, knowing he needed it.

With a smile as bright as a lighthouse beam, he'd say, "You're our angel, Lucy. We couldn't have wished for a more perfect child, could we, Love?"

In her tailored twin-set and smart skirt covered with a fresh apron, Mum pretended to dust the table, her fingers trembling as she adjusted a perfectly aligned framed photo of the three of us. Her wavy brown hair always fell softly around her freckled face, but in moments like this, her deep blue eyes clouded with something hidden, a sorrow she never voiced. "Lucy, you're all we've ever wanted or needed. Now, let's have a group hug."

Her voice was always soft yet firm, a practiced poise that came from years of managing emotions she kept locked away. She would smile brightly, but in those moments discussing more children, light never reached her eyes. When she hugged me, a faint scent of Estée Lauder filled my nose. And beneath the polished exterior was a woman who worried about everyone but herself.

We'd laugh, clinging to one another, happy to have dodged the painful topic once again. In time, it became a no-go area, and a few months after the last of these discussions, I got the best gift ever—Rufus, my faithful dog. He followed me everywhere, shared all my secrets, and completed our little family.

Maybe it was because I was an only child, but I grew up a little spoiled and a lot independent. I didn't share my toys, clothes, or time with others. I was old beyond my years, preferring books to people, and I never fitted in with other kids, with the exception of my best friend, Alice. I wasn't invited to parties, and I spent my school breaks reading in a quiet corner. Alice, shy and sweet, totally got me. She was my only ray of sunshine in a grey world.

My parents saw only the best in me, of course. They always did. I learned how to wrap them around my finger.

Mum would always say, "You deserve the best, Darling. Don't settle for less," as she tidied the house, her fingers brushing against the small tattoo of me. She'd cover it with makeup whenever she dressed up for an evening out, but it was always there—a mark of devotion on her leg that she never let anyone see.

To the outside world, I had it all. Anything I wanted, I got. Mum and Dad always said yes.

Then one day, Alice shunned me in the playground, hooking her arm through an older girl's and skipping away. The last grip I had on life began to slip. I felt alone, out of place—both with my family and among my peers. That's when the bulimia started. It gave me control, made me feel strong in at least one part of my life.

So why did I hate myself? Why did I have this constant need to rebel?

I was given everything—love, comfort, a future anyone would dream of. But instead of being grateful, a hollow space grew within me, restless and unfulfilled. Like I was chasing something no one else could see. Maybe that's why I pushed against it all, the perfect life they had built for me. I couldn't stand the pressure of being their perfect little girl. Maybe if I broke myself down first, no one else could.

By sixteen, I was skinny, a loner, and desperate to break free from the suffocating love of my parents. They worshipped me, placed me on a pedestal, but I needed to be someone different to what they wanted. I craved the rebellion they would never understand.

That's when I became a Goth. Black became my uniform—silk, velvet, leather, PVC, you name it. Occasionally, I'd throw on a splash of bold colour, but it was always dramatic, always meant to stand out. My soft-brown waves were dyed jet black, a transformation as sharp as my attitude. My freckles vanished beneath layers of thick foundation. A black septum ring gleamed, deep red lipstick made my lips unmissable, while dark eyeliner framed my blue eyes in a way that demanded attention. For the first time, I felt truly visible.

My voice was my ticket to a new world. I sang in the school choir, and my talent earned me an invitation into a group of like-minded creatives. We met every day at a disused railway station in Lapworth. I became lead singer for their band, *Black Maria*, alongside Jeff. He was older, mysterious, and I was soon hopelessly in love.

Jeff was twenty-two, wry and self-deprecating, with wild black hair, smeared lipstick, and smudged eyeliner that gave him an untouchable edge. His raspy voice and guitar skills made him unobtainable, way out of my league, but somehow, he saw something in me no one else did. And that was all that mattered.

Mum and Dad, of course, didn't approve. They despised the new me and my new boyfriend even more. One of the milder things they said was—"he needs a good wash."

I started coming home later and later. Eventually, I decided not to return at all. I stayed with Jeff at the station, sleeping rough among the graffiti-covered walls and piles of discarded spray cans. The place was a shrine to decades of youth culture, and I was in awe of it—the decay, the history, the freedom.

That became my life for the next six months.

My grades plummeted and with it my dreams of getting into a good university drifted further and further away. Mum and Dad begged me to come home.

"It's too cold for you to sleep rough," Mum pleaded. "Tell her, Patrick."

Dad nodded. "Your mum's right. Come back. You can bring Jeff if you want."

Mum's lips curled as she gave Dad a hostile glare.

I pouted. "She doesn't want him to come."

Dad glared at Mum, his hand balled into fists, his jaw tight. "Of course, Jeff's welcome."

Through gritted teeth, Mum forced a smile. "Yes, of course. Jeff can stay."

For a couple of weeks, we behaved. Jeff helped out around the house, mowing the lawn and pulling weeds, while I buried myself in my studies, pretending everything was normal. The garden was immaculate—straight lines, blooming roses—but inside, I was falling apart.

The bulimia crept back in, driven by that need for control. Beneath the surface, nothing felt right. My world was tilting, the ground shifting beneath me. I knew it wouldn't be long before everything spun out of control, leaving me tumbling through the chaos.

Always stoic, Mum hid her worry. "It's so good to have you home."

Dad agreed with a nod. "Yes, it's been far too long."

They were blind to the cracks forming beneath the surface.

Every day, Jeff would disappear for his walk back to the station, always growing more distant, more secretive. His excuse—he needed to see his friends. His eyes were bloodshot, his nose constantly running. I knew what was happening, but I tried to ignore it. Mum, of course, thought it was just hay fever.

I started skipping classes to accompany Jeff back to the station. I missed the place, the freedom it offered. But things had changed since we'd moved out. Wildflowers in jam jars now decorated every room, the smashed windows were repaired, and the sun streamed in, casting everything in a warm, golden glow.

Today as we strode along the deserted platform to the station house, a shiver ran down my back that had nothing to do with the autumn breeze. A premonition, maybe, that everything was about to change. Worried, I slipped my hand into Jeff's as we entered the building.

Then I saw her—a vision in a flowing pink dress. The kind that clung to her in the breeze, swirling around her legs like a dancer caught in motion. Her long, unkempt blonde hair was strewn with tiny wildflowers, giving her an ethereal, otherworldly air. Bracelets jangled on her wrists, layered with leather straps and woven beads as if she'd raided a festival stall.

She glided into the room, barefoot, radiating a carefree confidence that irritated me more than prickly heat. The thick scent of patchouli and incense followed her, overwhelming and cloying, hanging in the air like a statement. She walked straight up to Jeff, kissed him, and staked her claim. Her eyes told me everything—she wasn't just passing through.

Jeff stepped back with an awkward shrug. "Becky, this is Lucy. The girl I told you about. I'm staying with her parents."

My mind raced. *Where had I seen her before?*

She smiled, but her eyes were cold. "She's not what I expected."

I stiffened, a wave of anger wash over me.

Jeff let go of my hand. Shoving his in his pockets, he shared a secret smile with the detestable hippy.

I rushed outside, bile rising in my throat. As I heaved into the makeshift toilet, Becky's laughter echoed behind me, cruel and mocking.

I wiped my face, forcing myself to breathe. I won't let her take him. One thing's for sure—the hippy and I are never going to be friends. Quietly, I tiptoed to the window and watched them share a spliff, passing it back and forth, their heads close together, whispering God knows what. Tiny pricks of tears stung my eyes, but I gritted my teeth and refused to give them the satisfaction of seeing me upset.

When I stepped back into the room, I heard her whisper to Jeff, "I have a surprise for you later. Come back alone."

Jeff stubbed out the spliff they were sharing, grinding it into the floor. "You alright, Babe? You rushed out, and I wasn't sure if I should've come after you to check."

"Just a banging headache. Felt sick, that's all. I'm better now."

I slipped my arm around his waist, relieved for Becky's overpowering incense smell as it would cover any unpleasant smell that might be around me. "Let's go home. Leave Becky to carry on sprucing up the place."

I gave her a cold, dismissive look, up and down. "It looks… fabulous. You lot must be so proud. We'll come back soon to see how you're getting on. Will you still be here?"

Becky folded her arms, but Jeff shot her a look, silently warning her to keep quiet.

I dragged him outside, slamming the door behind us. One up for me.

We walked in silence, each wrapped in our own thoughts. I didn't trust Jeff, but I couldn't blame him entirely—I didn't expect anyone to treat me well. I thought about Becky. There was something about her—something familiar. She was full of life, colourful and natural, with a kind of wild, untouchable beauty. She reminded me of a girl I knew at school. But that Becky had dark hair and a darker mood, it couldn't be her.

"Race you to the park!" I tapped Jeff on the arm before sprinting ahead.

Jeff's lithe frame powered past me, his elbow catching me as we reached the tree. We tumbled onto the grassy bank and made love in a secluded spot, tangled in each other. For a moment, everything felt right. I was the girl he adored, still the Goth, wrapped up in the silent music of us.

Afterward, basking in a shared glow, I smiled, almost… at peace.

"I need a smoke."

"But you quit, you haven't touched one for months. Though you had one with Becky earlier…"

"Not cigarettes. A spliff." His voice sharpened. "Don't give me that look. Don't go all holier-than-thou on me."

"I'm not." I got up from the grass. "But we agreed, no spliffs, especially at my parents' house."

"Spliffs are nothing. Just a bit of weed. I used to inject worse, and you did too, if I remember right." His eyes narrowed, and he sneered, disgust clear in his voice. "You're such a bloody goody two-shoes these days."

Heart racing, my hands trembling, I took a step back. "But you promised…"

I didn't see it coming. His fist slammed into me, knocking me down. I hit the ground hard as the kicks followed, one after another, raining over my body. Curled up, shielding myself, each breath came in shallow gasps, my chest tight with fear. Panic gripped me so hard it felt like the air had been stolen from my lungs. Each new pain shocked my mind as well as my body.

"Get up, you crazy bitch!" he snarled, standing over me. "You deserved that. Stop crying or I'll head straight back to the station."

Through swollen eyes, I glanced around the park. Kids were playing in the distance, oblivious. My body ached, bruises already forming in deep purple patches. I could feel blood trickling down my chin.

Another accident, Dad would say. Shame coiled around me like a snake, squeezing the breath from my chest.

"Get up!" Jeff yanked at my hair, dragging me to my feet. "Someone's coming."

Wiping my face, I forced myself to breathe. I couldn't let her win—not like this. Reaching for the grassy bank, I grasped a clump of weeds, pulling myself up while brushing down my clothes. *This isn't the real Jeff, I've done this. This mess is my fault.*

I always made excuses for Jeff. It was my nagging, I told myself, that made him snap. He'd come around, apologise, and beg for my forgiveness like always. But right now, there was nothing—no reaction, no emotion. Just cold silence. I had to remember—it's all my fault, anyway. Despite everything, he was still the one I loved.

I reached up to touch him, hoping for a sign of forgiveness, some small gesture to make things right. After hesitating he took my hand, and I limped alongside him, smiling through the pain, scolding myself. I asked for this. I didn't deserve better.

Mum's eyes nearly popped out of her head. "My god! Lucy, what happened? Let me look at you."

Jeff jumped in before I could answer, his voice flat and rehearsed. "She's clumsy, aren't you, Babe? Fell down the embankment. Took two of us to pull her back up."

I avoided her gaze. "It's not as bad as it looks. I'll go upstairs and get changed."

Mum wasn't buying it. Her eyes flicked between Jeff and me, suspicion creeping in making her tone razor sharp. "How come you're not muddy, Jeff, if you helped her?"

Jeff shuffled, blind to her concern, already weaving his next lie. "My friend Becky got muddy. I held onto the lamppost so she could get to Lucy. Isn't that right, Babe?" His eyes locked onto mine, daring me to contradict him.

I swallowed hard, guilt for lying and shame weighing down on me making my words tremble. "Yeah, that's right, Mum."

An hour later, Dad came home from work. I could hear him and Mum whispering in the kitchen, voices hushed and strained. I held my breath until they stopped.

Mum called out, "Dinner's ready when you are."

At the table, Dad tried to make conversation as if everything was fine and completely ignored the bruises on my face and my limp. "How was your day?"

What could I say? Oh, you know, Dad, just the usual—got kicked around a bit, made excuses for Jeff, lied to Mum again. Instead, I forced a smile, pushing the words past the lump in my throat. "Fine. Just fine."

He turned his attention to Jeff. "If you've got time later, could you help me at the depot? I've got some deliveries to make."

"Sure, no problem. We'll leave the girls to chat. I'll head to the station on the way back, if that's okay with you, Babe?"

Something about his false concern and deference sent a spark of anger through me. His voice, soft and careful, played the part of the caring partner so perfectly that it almost fooled me—well almost. But I knew better. Beneath the surface, where my love for him burned, something darker festered. I hated how much I craved his approval, how the thought of losing him filled me with panic, yet I couldn't forget what had happened earlier.

"Yes of course. What time will you be back?" *What else could I say? Hey, if you so much as touch her I won't just boil a bunny!*

"Not sure. Don't wait up."

Don't wait up! What did that mean? My chest tightened. He planned to stay out late, probably with her... hippy Becky. Or maybe with someone else entirely—who knew how many women he was stringing along?

I nodded, trying to appear nonchalant, but inside, anger crumbled and self-loathing arose. I knew what he was doing, I knew he was slipping away, but what could I do? Confront him? He'd just twist it; make it like I was paranoid or clingy. *Maybe I am. Maybe I deserved this.*

A lump stuck in my throat, my head throbbed with unspoken fears. Why did I bother asking? I knew he wouldn't come home. And if he did, I'd just be waiting here, pretending everything was fine, pretending I wasn't dying inside.

I forced a smile and swallowed the knot in my throat. I couldn't lose him. Not yet. Not like this.

Dad returned around nine o'clock, grabbed a beer, and went straight upstairs for a bath. I sat alone, restless and worried, unable to shake the dread creeping up my spine.

In the morning, Jeff still hadn't come back. By noon, my anxiety was unbearable. Borrowing Mum's car, I drove to the old station though I could have run there in fifteen minutes.

Switching off the engine I heard familiar sounds: laughter, the jingle of glasses, and Lance's guitar strumming. As I entered the building, I lost myself in the music and the memories of belonging. But then reality crashed in, and I burst into the waiting room. Two guys were shooting up, another eating Coco Pops. Lance was hunched over, head down.

"Has anyone seen Jeff? He didn't come home last night." My voice sounded feeble even to me.

Lance concentrated on rolling his next spliff. The others, high and delirious, laughed about red shoes and Tonto, oblivious to my desperation.

With frustration boiling over I clenched my teeth. "Come on, you're not in the Masons. Has anyone seen him?"

Lance glanced up, adjusting his glasses. "I've not been around much and I've not seen him in days, which is odd for him, he normally searches me out. Guess he's been busy… if you know what I mean, wink wink."

"Where's Becky?" Dreading the answer my fists clenched and unclenched.

He shrugged, polishing his glasses. "She split last night. Said this place was a waste of her time and headed to London. No one's missing the incense, but she was easy on the eyes, if you know what I mean."

The guys erupted in laughter. Nothing able to break their drug-induced haze.

My voice cracked as I fought back tears. "If you see Jeff, tell him to come home."

Lance's tone softened as he took in my lumps and bruises. "Wouldn't waste your breath on him. He's a player, and he's got a temper to match. You deserve better." He paused and threw me a wink. "I'd give you a ride anytime if you want a real man."

I had to get out. I couldn't stay there, not with them laughing, not with all those reminders of how I'd lost him. *My sanctuary…* but it wasn't mine anymore, was it? Tears blurred my vision as I ran, hitting the tracks beneath my feet, as if they could lead me anywhere but here.

Standing by the disused tracks, I stared at the storm brewing in the sky. *Even the clouds were angry,* I thought, watching them eat away at the hills I used to love. But the darkness? Somehow, it suited me. For the first time in days, my breath slowed, and I let a small, bitter smile tug at my lips. Maybe this was what I deserved.

Driving home later, I clung to the wheel, the silenced stretch out and emptiness expanded within me. Parked on the drive, I found myself staring at the door, hoping—no, needing—him to come back. He had to show up. He always did. He'd be sorry. He'd fix this. But I went inside alone.

As the days passed, my bruises healed. And with each fading mark, my hope for him dimmed too. But even after everything, I knew I'd take him back in a heartbeat. What did that say about me? A hollow laugh escaped my lips. *I'm that desperate.*

Chapter 3

Lucy—Three Years Later

"STRAIGHT A'S! Who would've thought?" Nancy beamed, adjusting her new 1920s cloche style blue felt hat.

Patrick puffed on a cigar and tapped his feet to the music. "Yes, seeing her surrounded by friends and getting a job offer from Hargrove & Collins it's more than we hoped for."

"It's been over three years since you-know-who left; I think I can stop worrying about him coming back now—and good riddance to him."

"Forget him, Nancy. He's gone, and Lucy's got Jordan now. She's happy, and he's a great guy—his dad's a professor at Cambridge, after all. What more could we ask for?" Patrick's smile stretched ear to ear. "Not bad for business either."

"I suppose. And they do appear to be happy together."

*****

I skipped over to Mum and Dad, arm in arm with Jordan. Happy at last, I'd become a new person, comfortable in my own skin. Soft flattering makeup, natural brown hair bouncing in waves past my shoulders, and casual, comfortable clothes made me unrecognizable from the Goth I had been. Reinvented, confident, with a fresh coat of self-assurance, I was the star of my own show.

Jordan, completely smitten, carried his 'lucky poker chip' everywhere to remind him of the day we met.

*****

Remembering how we met was one of my favourite pastimes often drifting back to that night at the school prom. It was the happiest day of my life. I'd arrived with Adam, a friend of mine, and Jordan had been with his twin sister, Julie. As soon as I saw him across the dance floor, my heart skipped a beat. Tall, tanned, with jet-black hair and the most infectious smile I'd ever seen. He was a vision of strength. I turned away, a guy like him wouldn't be interested in me.

Adam nudged me, "Here comes Jordan and Julie! Let's say hi. I've fancied Julie since grade three, but we were always in different forms."

I hesitated, my heart thudding in my chest.

Adam beckoned them over. "Jordan, meet Lucy."

Jordan's eyes lit up with a smile that could light the room.

Adam hooked his arm around Julie's shoulder. "Let me buy you a drink."

The two of them left chatting away, but Jordan stayed behind. "Hello beautiful."

Blushing, I smoothed my lilac dress, trying not to show how flustered I was. Was this happening?

"I'm Jordan," he extended his hand. "Do you play poker?"

I laughed. "That's the worst chat-up line I've ever heard!"

His laugh was deep and genuine. "So, that's a yes?"

We spent the night playing poker, talking, laughing. I was buzzing with nervous energy, riding the high of what might be, and it wasn't long before our late-night study sessions turned into something more. Jeff was a distant memory. I'd found my soul mate in Jordan.

*****

Three years at university passed in a blur of happiness. And then we were at my graduation from Oxford, with a degree in finance. Jordan graduated with a first in maths from Cambridge.

Our celebratory meal had an odd vibe that I couldn't put my finger on, but I was bubbling with excitement because Jordan had suggested we move in together. I could have flown and danced with the stars, and returned on a comet I was that high. We'd have our own space—no more shared student accommodations with maggots in the kitchen and mouldy leftovers.

Mum and Dad surprised us.

"We'd like to buy your first home in Earlswood, Solihull."

Jordan and I looked at each other in shock.

"Go on, let us," Dad insisted. "We want you to live close to us, and you'll both be able to commute to Birmingham for your jobs, it's not far."

Mum pulled out the house details from her handbag and passed them to us. "Here's the one we've found. Try to see beyond what it looks like now. It has promise, lots of it."

Jordan appeared genuinely overwhelmed by the offer. "Wow, it's fantastic isn't it."

A week later, we went to see the house on Sycamore Lane. The moment I stepped inside, the worn charm of the Victorian detached caught my eye, though the peeling paint and cracked windows echoed tales of neglect. With the loft conversion it had become an extra spacious three-storey living space.

The garden stretched wild and untamed, yet underneath the tangled mess, I could imagine its beauty. Beyond it, the shimmering Earlswood Lakes peeked through, drawing Jordan's gaze. His grin lit up the moment he saw them, and I couldn't help but wrap my arms around Mum and Dad, warmth and gratitude spreading through me like sunlight after a storm.

"You're amazing," I breathed, fighting back the lump in my throat. "But can you afford this?"

Dad chuckled, his eyes twinkling as he grinned at Jordan. "For our favourite girl—and maybe her future husband—anything's possible."

Jordan's cheeks flushed, his hand reaching out to shake Dad's. "Patrick, let's not jump ahead. I haven't proposed... yet."

Everything felt perfect then, like we were standing on the edge of something extraordinary. I was yet to learn... the higher you climb, the harder you fall.

For half a year, the days blurred together in a haze of dust, paint, and arguments, as the house transformed—and my relationship with Jordan crumbled.

The entrance now gleamed, vast enough to fit a family of giraffes, though I'd never let them trample across the pristine tiled floor and under floor heating. The stairway, now sleek with glass panels and chrome fittings, spiralled upward to the second and third floors, doors towering in every direction.

Sash windows, their frames scarcely touched by the plain roller blinds, opened up to a panorama of seagulls, ducks, and sailboats dotting Earlswood Lakes. A breath-taking view that, despite its beauty, felt as distant as Jordan had become—each day pulling him further from me, even when we were standing side by side.

Over those six months of renovations, Jordan's frustration had deepened, stretching the gap between us. In the beginning, he had welcomed my parents' help, nodding along to their ideas and plans. But as time went by, he changed. What once was polite agreement turned into silent resentment. My parents' advice, though well-meant, started to feel like meddling to him, and he started to withdraw. Little by little, he had become harder to reach.

"When are they going to hand over the deeds to us?" he'd seethed one day.

"I don't know, love. Maybe when we get married."

Red flared up his neck and consumed his face with its heat. "Blackmail then… 'Marry our daughter if you want the house we said we were buying for you!' How cheap does that make you?"

"They don't mean it like that, I'm sure. They've either forgotten or they plan it as gift sometime in the future."

"I feel like an interloper in my own home. It's embarrassing. Ask them why they haven't given them to us yet."

I shook my head.

"You're pathetic!"

That had been one of many such discussions. Each day quiet sighs turned into cutting remarks, until I couldn't remember a time when he wasn't berating me for being stupid and pathetic.

One afternoon, while we were talking about the final touches on the living room, he snapped. His face tightened, and before I could react, he stood, the chair scraping harshly against the floor. He came up to me with his fist clenched and I shrunk back. I could see he was seething and tensed expecting to be hit. It didn't happen that day. Without a word, he stormed out, slamming the door behind him. On future occasions, when my parents weren't in the next room, he wouldn't hold back.

After one of his tantrums, Mum and Dad exchanged concerned glances, but I shrank away from explaining. Chewing over a thousand unvoiced thoughts, I just sat there. In the end, the gramophone of my internal monologue settled on two beliefs: *It's my fault. I have to be better.*

Jordan's anger only grew from there. Every time my parents visited, he'd grumble, "Not them again," before slamming the back door and disappearing—to the squash courts or the pub with his friends. I'd cover for him, making up stories about sudden work calls or friends in need. My parents never pushed for answers, but their confusion was clear. They tried to fill the growing void with gifts and praise, but every well-meaning gesture from them enraged Jordan more.

He couldn't afford the expensive things they gave me, so those gifts were quickly hidden away to escape his anger. But tension already gripped every part of our lives. My jittery hands trembled at the smallest sound. The house, once full of hope, now seemed cold and vast, as if it belonged to someone else. Jordan spent most of his time out, consumed by late nights at the firm in his relentless push to make partner.

I tried to keep up appearances, cooking elaborate meals for his colleagues when they came over, but we were never invited back. It wasn't long before Jordan's criticisms turned personal. "My colleagues can tell something's wrong with us," he'd sneer. "They don't like you, and they don't admire you."

I'd shout back, "What's wrong with me, then?"

Through clenched teeth, he'd growl, "You dress like your mother, and you're holding me back."

The words cut deep. I tried to remember the early years at university—when we laughed together and had our own secret language of love. I clung to those memories, desperate to believe we could find our way back. It had to be my fault he was angry all the time and I lived in fear that he'd leave.

I gave up my job when Dad offered to support me with an allowance. For a while, that had helped. I found pieces of myself again, wearing makeup to hide not just the emotional bruises, but the physical ones too. I joined a local badminton club and made a few friends at the Tanworth-in-Arden coffee group.

But none of it helped. We just limped along.

One night, the door slammed. "Honey, I'm home!" He took the stairs two at a time. "I hope you're ready for me." Sarcasm had become one of his sharpest tools.

I cowered as he climbed in beside me. He reeked of garlic and sweat from his gym session. There was no tenderness left in him. As he entered me, I fought to hold back my tears, thinking of the love we used to share. This was nothing like that. The distance between had become an ocean, vast and cold. I felt unattractive and unloved.

"You're as useless as a wooden statue," he hissed when he finished taking his pleasure with brutal force. "No wonder I can't be bothered with you."

He wrinkled his nose, clenched his fists and thumped me—careful to leave no marks on my face... as always. Finished with defiling me, and not wanting to be near me, Jordan went into the other bedroom and slammed the door. He never slept with me anymore. The sense of abandonment hurt more than my aching ribs, arms, and legs.

Tears stung my eyes as I buried my face in the pillow. "You're a monster," I sobbed, voice trembling. "I'm not your punch bag." I fell asleep weeping… yet again.

Every night I dreaded his return. Would he be drunk today? Or would my soft, lovable Jordan emerge from the pits he'd disappeared into?

Each time Monster-Jordan attacked me, I told myself it was my fault. *Who wants their in-laws interfering all the time anyway?* It's on me that I don't make him feel like the man of the house.

Months slipped by. The house stood finished—a modern, sterile space, lacking warmth, devoid of laughter, a reflection of our empty lives.

The more distant Jordan became, the more I became a ghost in my own home. The old habit of stress-vomiting returned, and I became a jittery shell of myself losing my grip on reality.

Jordan's rage worsened. No longer caring who saw, his fists left bruises I had to hide with makeup. Although Dad offered me an allowance when I'd quit my job, it hadn't eased the growing tension between us. For a while, it helped. I reconnected with a couple of girlfriends from uni, joined a badminton club, and tried to regain some confidence. Nothing worked.

The cycle of violence continued, and I sunk to a place where I became too terrified to leave him. *How could I exist without him? Where would I go and what would I do? Nobody else would have me.* It never occurred to me that I believed this solely because it was what he told me several times a day.

Every punch, every insult, I told myself I deserved. I wanted him to love me again, to be the Jordan I once knew. But deep down, I knew that man had gone.

Trapped, desperately trying to survive in a relationship that was killing me.

And now a new stage—the silent treatment. He refused to talk to me except when he was barking orders. I had become a second-class citizen, no worse than that—I was the lowest of the low, not worth acknowledging. I retreated into a shell. I couldn't go out anymore and didn't answer calls from anyone except Mum and Dad. I ordered groceries online and made the driver leave them on the step so no one would see me. I was ashamed. I was lost. I was broken.

Today, Jordan flipped the lucky poker chip up in the air, caught it and then tossed it in the bin. Without a word he had told me he was done with me.

*****

A few days later, Mum turned up unannounced, her face flushed as she breezed into the hallway. "Hello, Darling! We're off for a spa day, you and me. A little break for us girls. Your dad's paying." Her cheerfulness seemed out of place, and I stood there in my grubby dressing gown, clutching my teddy bear, mascara smudged around my eyes.

"I can't today, Mum. I'm cleaning the house," I mumbled, knowing the lie wouldn't hold.

Mum, always the sharp-eyed matriarch, went to set her handbag down but missed the hall table. It clattered onto the floor with a thud. Her expression softened as she took in the mess, her voice gentle but firm. "What's happening here? Don't tell me to mind my own business. I've known for a while now that something's wrong. Look at you. This isn't you. Please, stop crying."

As soon as she wrapped her arms around me, I broke down, sobbing uncontrollably. "Mum, it's all gone wrong. I can't fix it."

"What's happened?"

"My hormones have gone crazy and the estrogen patches aren't working. I'm all over the place. I can't keep the house clean. Everything gets on top of me." The acceptance of failure heaped upon me and I crumbled under it, utterly defeated.

Mum, ever the optimist, opened the bedroom door, but the sight—and smell—stopped her in her tracks. Dirty sheets, clothes scattered everywhere, and the dust so thick it coated the furniture. I saw her grimace as the musty stench hit her.

I rushed to hide the mouldy apple cores littering the bed and tried to cover the bloodstains that screamed my shame. "Mum, please leave."

But she wasn't having it. "No, not this time," she shook her head. "I'll send Janet and her team over to clean for you. You go and throw on some clothes, and we'll head to the spa."

There's no way I'm letting you see my body. "Mum, I can't go there. It's not my thing anymore. Let's just go for lunch at Morton's."

Her confusion flickered for a moment, but she didn't push. Instead, she took me into her arms, and I let the tears flow again, my body aching for answers I couldn't find. As she hummed the familiar lullaby from my childhood, a fleeting calm washed over me. I clung to it, desperate for anything to soothe the storm inside.

True to her word, Mum phoned Janet and pulled a few favours. Twenty minutes later a brigade of three turned up armed with buckets of cleaning materials. Leaving home with wet hair but fresh in a clean jumper and jeans, I shrank into myself, hating what the cleaners would think of me.

Morton's music filtered over our heads as we sat across from each other in the restaurant. The food on my plate went untouched and Mum's eyes kept flicking from the plate to my face. "So, what's making you so sad? I'm really worried about you."

"I'm okay, Mum. Just a bit lost now that the house is done." It was a lie, and we both knew it, but I couldn't bring myself to say more. Instead, I focused on pushing food around my plate as my heart raced. My body trembled with the effort of keeping the truth buried.

Mum's eyes welled up, but she didn't press further. She just nodded, her hand resting on mine, trying to offer comfort where words couldn't.

That night, Jordan came in with his hands on his hips, his eyes dark and narrowed. He looked around the now spotless house and sneered. "Who did this? Not you, that's for sure. You're a lazy cow."

The thuds of my quickened heartbeat pounded in my ears as fear twisted inside me. "I-I did it. It t-t-took all day."

To my surprise, that night he was gentler than usual, and for a moment, I let myself believe things might change. I floated on that fragile hope, smiling through the cracks, clapping my hands, and crossing my fingers for luck, praying that this time, life would return to some version of normal.

*****

A few days passed, and I was lulled into a false sense of security. I certainly didn't see it coming.

An early morning dream dissolved as pain registered. A scream left my mouth before I opened my eyes. With one punch, Jordan sent me flying off the bed to land in a heap on the floor.

His footsteps vibrated through the floorboards and I scrambled to get up. Before I could, he kicked me in the ribs. I doubled over, moaning. "That's for not having my breakfast ready, you lazy cow!"

Whimpering, I used the bed to pull myself up. "I'll get it now."

Jordan's grip on my arm was sudden, vice-like. I staggered, breath catching, tumbling into my worst nightmare.

He yanked the wardrobe door open. "Get in there, be quiet, and don't move. I'll let you out when I get back from work." His shower-wet hair dripped onto the floor, each drop echoing in the silence.

I stared at the growing puddle at his feet, my body trembling. Any protest, any sign of defiance, would make things worse. His punishments had grown more creative lately, and the thought of what might come next froze me. My breath quickened, uneven, my heart hammered my ribs. The darkness ahead swallowed me whole as he shoved me inside. The wardrobe doors closed with a dull click, followed by the unmistakable sound of the key turning in the lock.

Minutes later, the front door slammed. The car engine revved, tyres crunching on the gravel outside. Silence.

I wept uncontrollably, eyes fixed on the thin cracks of light under the doors, each one mocking me. In the cramped darkness, I curled into myself, my bruised skin scraping against the sharp edges of hangers and shoes. My fingers trembled as they brushed over the familiar shapes of my leather handbags, now useless relics in this prison.

The silence pressed in on me, suffocating. A ticking time bomb; not the pain, nor the darkness, or even the confined space—injustice made me explode. I screamed, over and over, desperate for someone to hear. But no one would. No one ever heard me scream in our delectable detached Victorian. Only Jordan, my soul mate turned tormentor.

Time slipped by in jagged fragments. My thoughts spiralled. He wouldn't leave me here, would he? This was a trick. He'd come back, laughing, teasing me for being so scared. But as the seconds stretched into minutes, reality hit me like a slap. He'd left me. He wasn't coming back until he decided he was ready. Panic took over and I hammered the door until my hands were too bruised to continue.

With my head in my hands, wild thoughts dragged me down into a pit of despair. Clawing my way out of it, I resumed my attack on our made-to-measure wardrobe doors with my feet this time.

Each jerk caused pain to shoot through me. Ten minutes of fruitless kicking sent me into sobs of self-pity. *Where's Ted?* Frantic for comfort, I tore at the shoe boxes but when I couldn't find him, I put my head back and howled.

Time elapsed, I didn't know how much but it dawned on me that this was no trick; Jordan wasn't coming to let me out until he returned from work. *What if he doesn't come home?* Terror, raw and dreadful consumed me as I imagined myself becoming a skeleton in my perfect bedroom fittings.

I needed to concentrate and think of a way to get out. *But how?* My breath came in ragged gasps and sweat dripped down my back though my hands were freezing. My mind raced, searching for something—anything.

My phone! Maybe it was still on the bedside table.

Fearing the monster was waiting downstairs to torment me, I mumbled, "Alexa, call Mum." The faint cry for help got swallowed up in the thick silence of the empty house.

Nothing happened. No AI response, no ringtone, and no steps running up the stairs. Jordan had gone. If he was still here, he'd already be gloating, standing outside the wardrobe mocking me. I put my mouth close to the door and shouted. "Alexa, call Mum!"

The ringing tone broke the silence, sharp and sudden. My heart skipped a beat and started racing.

"Hello, Darling. Lovely to hear from you," Mum's voice floated through the air.

Tears streamed down my face as I cried into the darkness, "Help me, Mum. Please."

"Lucy? What's wrong? Are you okay?" Her voice grew louder, panicked. "Where are you? I can't hear you, speak up!"

"I'm locked in the wardrobe," I choked out, sobbing. "Can you get me out?" I yelled with a bit more force.

"I'm on my way. Hang in there, you're a brave girl. I love you."

Minutes felt like hours as I waited, curled into a ball, listening for the sound of her car. I nearly passed out from relief when I heard the front door unlock, and then her footsteps, heavy and urgent, racing up the stairs.

"Lucy, are you in there?"

I heard the panic in her voice. "Yes, but I'm scared, Mum. Hurry, he could come back any second."

Her voice grew sharper, angrier. "Has that bastard taken the key?"

I whimpered, my words choking me. "I think so. He took it out and I didn't hear him put it down." My hands shook, counting in my head, trying to block out the darkness. One, two, three, four... I repeated over and over like a prayer—my attempt to block the terror of the confined space.

"Stay with me, Lucy. I'll use his baseball bat. Does he still keep it under the bed?"

"Yes, hurry, Mummy." The sounds of Mum shuffling around didn't ease my palpitations. Shrinking back into the corner I put my head on my knees and covered it with my hands.

The first crack of the bat against the door knob made me jump. The door rattled with each of Mum's mighty blows. The door handle crashed to the floor on the twentieth whack. Mum yanked the door open and light poured in causing me to blink at the sudden brightness.

Mum stood there, panting, bat in hand, sweat rolling down her face. She looked like my personal superhero.

She pulled me out, and I collapsed into her arms, her familiar scent wrapping around me like a safety blanket. My body shook with sobs as words tumbled from my mouth, each one a bullet tearing through the years of silence. The bruises hidden beneath my clothes, the terror that had become my daily companion—all of it laid bare in front of her.

Mum's face hardened, her eyes narrowing into slits. "He's going, Lucy. He's not staying another day."

I nodded, numb, exhausted, but a flicker of hope ignited somewhere deep inside me. As Mum threw his clothes into black bin bags, she rang Dad, updating him.

"Lucy, are you alright?" Dad's voice trembled through the phone, heavy with guilt.

"I'm sorry, Dad. I didn't want you to find out. I'm so ashamed."

His voice cracked. "We knew something wasn't right, but we had no idea. I promise you; he'll pay for this. I thought it odd when he bought a knob-lock instead of a storage lock for that cupboard. When I questioned him about it, he blurted out some drivel about buying the wrong one and what did it matter. I could kill him."

I passed the phone back to Mum. "I need to save my strength for Jordan. Let's end this now."

Mum nodded; determination etched into her face. "We're going to his work."

Dad's voice came through the line again, "I've never been prouder of you girls."

We drove towards Birmingham in silence, my heart pounding with a mix of fear and adrenaline. Mum's calm steadied me as we pulled into the car park.

Charging past the receptionist, we went straight into the open-plan office.

"Hello, Lucy, long time no see," Ned, one of Jordan's colleagues, said as we approached. "Has Jordan forgotten his lunch?"

Lifting my chin, I pushed back my hair to reveal black and purple bruises across my left cheek and neck. "He's going to wish it was just his lunch. Where is he?"

"Went into a meeting ages ago, he's…"

Jordan appeared and on seeing me and Mum, he froze.

Mum scowled and dropped the bin bags on the floor. "Talk of the devil."

The room blurred until all I could see were Jordan's clenched fists. Suddenly scared, I cowered. Anger and fear blended until I didn't know which emotion was causing me to shake.

Jordan tried to play it cool in front of his colleagues, "Not now, Lucy. I'm busy. I'll ring you later."

I almost ran, but Mum's hand touched my elbow, it was all I needed. I stepped forward, my voice muted but dripping with venom. "You locked me in a wardrobe this morning and left me there. You know I'm terrified of the dark. Mum had to break the door down with your baseball bat."

Jordan's face turned beetroot red. "That's a lie!"

"Before you sink any further into lies, you should be aware that Mum set her phone to record while getting me out of the wardrobe as evidence for the police."

The room fell silent, all eyes on Jordan.

His bravado faltered. "Lucy, I'd never..."

Although my voice was quiet, strength and courage grew inside me. "You've been controlling me since the day we met. But no more. That's why I'm here. I've finally seen the light. We're over. Don't come home."

His colleagues exchanged uneasy glances, some shaking their heads in disgust. His boss, Helen, stood up, her eyes blazing. "Jordan, conference room. Now."

Jordan's world crumbled around him as he walked away. Free at last, I'd never be his victim again. Relief came so hard that I started shaking uncontrollably. Mum wrapped her cardigan around me like a shield.

Michael jumped up and offered me his chair. In moments, his work colleagues who I thought detested me, rushed around all-consoling.

"Always knew he was a piece of shit," hissed Michael shaking his head. "Why on earth did you stay with him?"

I ignored that question; that deep, revealing answer would need addressing before I could ever talk to anyone about it.

"He told me you all hated me."

"It's so not true. Each time we saw you together we were worried about you. We couldn't say anything for fear of what Jordan might do."

I gave in to sobs, no longer embarrassed, just relieved.

Michael passed me a box of tissues. "Trust me, he'll never bother you again."

Dabbing at my face with a tissue, I nodded. It would be impossible for me to be a bigger mess but I glanced at Mum and smiled. I realised that my life was never going to be the same again.

I had been saved by Super-Mum and myself! Elated, I left the office punching the sky. The handcuffs were finally off.

Chapter 4

Lucy—Healing & Dealing

JORDAN'S DISAPPEARANCE had been swift and absolute, like a wisp of smoke snatched away by the wind. No fight, no demands, no backward glance at me as he faded into my past.

His colleagues told me he vanished before the company could fire him. No one had heard from him since. His parents, who had once been so proud of him, had lost contact too. To me, Jordan had dissolved into a bad dream, a shadow I kept waking from in a cold sweat—never sure if he was real or just the product of my fears.

I couldn't return to our house in Earlswood. His presence still reverberated through the walls, with a silence insufferable and mocking. Instead, I clung to the safety of Mum and Dad's detached in Lapworth, as though their presence could piece together the fragments of my shattered life.

Even there, stepping outside felt like walking into a minefield. The sound of footsteps behind me sent me into a cold sweat. My heart would race, my skin prickling with panic, until I sprinted back to the house. The closer the footsteps got, the more my throat tightened, and my voice vanished. Every time, I'd hammer on the door, desperate, my cries trapped inside.

Dad, ever protective, would scan the street with steely eyes, making sure it was just some harmless passer-by. Mum would pull me close, my face pressed against her chest as she rocked me until fear drained away, leaving me hollow but safe.

But after months of this, I saw the toll it was taking. Mum's once-bright eyes had dulled, her laugh now a rare sound. Dad's protective instincts had morphed into something suffocating. He was always checking my location, tracking my every move.

'Find My Friend' had become my invisible leash. I couldn't breathe. Every step monitored, my world shrinking around me.

And Dad? He found solace at the pub, downing pint after pint, stumbling through the door in the early hours, smelling of beer, smoke, and sometimes cheap perfume. I knew something was broken between him and Mum. Their hushed debates grew sharper, their arguments subdued but more frequent. Dad had started cutting corners at work, letting go of employees who'd been loyal for years. The cracks were showing. And I knew it was because of me.

The realisation hit me like a punch to the gut: I had to go. For their sake, if not mine. They needed space to rebuild their lives, to focus on saving the business. I couldn't drag them down with me anymore.

Selling the house in Earlswood felt like a small offering, a token to help them stay afloat. Dad insisted on finishing the patio before we listed it as if some fresh stonework could bury the memories trapped inside. When it sold, Mum and Dad grew lighter, with old friends returning—those who had drifted away during the tense days and heavy moods, now eager to rekindle their bond. Laughter slowly found its way back into their lives.

With the sale behind us, I started making my own plans. I couldn't stay at home with them, tethered to the past. London appealed to me—a place where I could disappear into the crowd, just another face among millions. No one would gossip about me there. No one would know what I'd been through.

I found a job bartending at 'The Al-Chemist,' a trendy spot in Canary Wharf. It was a stopgap, a way to keep my hands busy, my mind distracted. I bleached my hair platinum blonde, cut it into a sharp bob, and embraced a Bohemian style that gave me a new identity. With sparkly blue eye shadow and a thick black eyeliner swirl I had an almost sixties style. 'Lu,' they called me now. I'd filled out a bit—back to a size ten—but the emotional scars remained, a fading echo of the life I'd survived.

Behind the bar, I became a different person. I mastered the art of molecular mixology, earning rave reviews for my elaborate, theatrical cocktails. People came from all over just to watch me work, their faces lighting up as I performed. It felt good, disappearing into this new persona, this new life.

The loft in Dalston became my sanctuary. A converted synagogue with high ceilings and light streaming in through the windows, it was far removed from the shadows of Birmingham. The tree-lined street reminded me of home, but it was different enough that I could breathe here. I rented it with the help of my parents' generosity, but it was mine. My space. My life.

And then, one day, scrolling through Craigslist, something caught my eye. A headline: 'Charlie, sniff and coke £50.' A mobile number. A click away. It was absurd how easy it was.

I met Daniel that same day in a café in Hackney. He walked in like he owned the place—over six feet tall, dressed like he'd just come from the gym. He spotted me immediately.

"You must be Lu," he said, a grin tugging at his lips.

"How di-di-did you know?" I stuttered, sweat beading on my forehead.

"Just a guess. You're tapping the table and sweating. It's freezing in here." His deep, smooth voice sent a wave of desire over me. Deep brown eyes locked with mine, he winked. My stomach flipped.

He slid the package across the table, our hands brushing. His touch was warm, his presence disarming. "I'll see you again, Lu. Take it easy."

"Thanks, Daniel. I will." I watched him walk away, admiring his swagger, the way his curly hair caught the light. A thrill shot through me; this wasn't just business anymore.

Anticipation and possibility gave me a natural high as I half-walked, half-skipped all the way back to the loft flat.

That night, I let the not-so-natural high wash over me, every nerve tingling with alertness, power surging through my veins.

Waves of longing swelled inside me, crashing with frustration—there was no one to call. I missed Jeff, the way his touch could stir something deep, and how our nights stretched into conversations that seemed endless. *Why did Becky have to ruin it all? We had been happy until she'd come along.*

The memory blurred like the edge of a dream slipping away. I wanted more—more of this warmth, more of us, more of what we used to be. Even if the truth stayed buried beneath that old, familiar haze, I chose to remember the parts that made me feel whole.

I searched the internet in a sudden frenzy. I couldn't find Jeff anywhere. On Facebook, Becky had posted pictures of herself with another man. *I knew they wouldn't last!* I couldn't help grinning.

As I was searching for Jeff, Daniel kept popping into my mind.

I giggled—the senseless almost frantic laugh that only drugs could induce—making me laugh when what I needed was an outlet for my frustration. Scanning the room for something to take out my frustration on, my eyes landed on Ted, the tattered teddy I'd tossed onto the bed earlier. Without thinking, I shouted, "Rock, Paper, Scissors, Shoot!" My fist balled into a rock, crushing Ted's imaginary scissors.

"You've lost, Ted." I hurled him at the door.

Ted lay there, silent as ever, his stuffing leaking out from every seam, one eye missing, the other hanging on by a single thread. Years of offering comfort and enduring these ridiculous games had taken their toll. He once looked pristine after trips to Mum's 'First Aid Station.' Now he was a mess, worn and threadbare, caught in the wrong place at the right time.

I paused, stretching out the moment. A clownish grin spread across my face. I knew what I'd do next. Grabbing my phone, I scrolled through Craigslist and dialled a number. Reckless me was back. With no parents peering over my shoulder a rush of daredevil burst out.

Sexy-Lucy took over, her voice soft and seductive. "Daniel, I need to see you. Where are you? I want you now."

"Who's this?"

Who is this, indeed? Honestly, I'm not so sure myself. I sprawled across the bed, drawing out each word. "It's me, Lu. We met this morning."

"That's right, the tapper who sweats a lot. I can tell you're smiling."

"I'm happy, I guess." My voice turned playful, high-pitched. "That's me, guilty as charged. You'll have to handcuff me, officer!"

"Do you need more coke, Lu?"

"Maybe. But I need you more… if you know what I mean."

"Where do you live?"

"Lucky End, Longmore Road, Dalston."

"I'll try to get away. I'll text you."

Flushed, I slammed my fist on the bedside table. The thud echoed through the room.

Thud… thud. "Shut up! We've got a baby trying to sleep down here," a voice from below shouted.

"Sorry," I mouthed at the ceiling, necking the rest of the bottle of red wine.

I turned my attention to the internet, fingers typing furiously as I searched for Jeff. He had to be out there somewhere, right?

Later that night, my phone pinged. *I'll be there in thirty minutes. Just getting dressed.*

A grin curled my lips. I hadn't lost it after all.

Rushing to get ready, I scrubbed the wine stains from my teeth, my reflection grinned back at me with twinkling eyes. I looked like the cat who got the cream, anticipation coursing through me until my body ached with want.

Daniel was a dream—early thirties, West Indian decent, with dark hair begging to be touched and brown eyes deep enough to drown in. My friends would call him 'sex on legs.'

I did a search to find out more about him and found him on Facebook. The account wasn't very old and didn't have a lot of content just the basic information and a few recent photographs. He was a PE teacher at a local school, and I guessed he dabbled in coke to keep his edge sharp or earn extra money. *Maybe tonight, I'll be the spark to his flame.*

After a quick shower, Ann Summers' silk lingerie wrapped around my skin like a second layer as lust filled my eyes. "Irresistible?" Today the mirror was my friend. "Abso-bloody-lutely!"

Twenty minutes later, a knock came at the door. I opened it, and his presence overwhelmed me, his masculinity setting fire to the place between my legs. My mouth went dry as heat rose to my cheeks, and I wished I hadn't drunk so much wine.

The room appeared smaller with him in it, his frame making everything else shrink. My hands trembled as I poured him a glass of wine. When I passed it to him, our fingers brushed. A fuse lit in my brain, exploding in sparks.

We moved to the bedroom, hand in hand. I kicked Ted aside with a grin. I was glad he had only one eye and no mouth tonight.

*****

Morning light filtered through the curtains. I blinked awake, reaching over to find Daniel already gone. Ted sat in the corner, silent, but something about him made me think he was grinning.

Irritated, I ripped out his remaining eye and flushed it down the toilet. Mum wouldn't be able to fix him now. *Why do I keep you around anymore?*

A note sat by the kettle, along with some coke.

Had to go, I play rugby at St. Peter's, noon. Join me if you're free. Daniel x

It was 11:30. Elated, I rushed into the bathroom for a quick shower before fishing Ted's eye from the toilet. Thankfully, it was still there. I re-stuffed him with straw that had fallen out and promised to sew the eye back on later. He deserved better after all the times he'd been there for me. *I don't know what gets into me sometimes.*

At the rugby field, I spot Daniel straight away. He stood out like a beacon, squatting in his white rugby shirt and red shorts, warming up with his teammates.

"So, this is why you didn't pick me up this morning," said a voice from beside me. I turned to see Pete, who it turned out was one of Daniel's teammates.

"Sure is." Daniel gave me a peck on the cheek.

Flushing bright red, I smiled. "I'm Lu. Nice to meet you. It's cold today. Who are you playing?"

"Leicester St Jude's. Come for a drink at the Lord Jim afterward. We usually head there when we play at home."

He pointed me toward a group of girls on the side-line. "The other girlfriends are over there if you want to join them. Clubhouse is behind them if you need a coffee."

Warmth spread through me as I hung onto the word 'girlfriend.' "Sounds good to me." I walked over in a daze, the glow from his words still clinging to me.

"Welcome to the cheerleaders. I'm Rebecca, Pete's other half," one of the girls said, gesturing to the group. "This is Pru, Carol, Pat, Sally, and Jazz."

"Thanks, awesome to meet you all. I'm Lu. I don't know anything about rugby, so I'll need all the help I can get."

Jazz smiled, patting the camping chair beside her. "Daniel's never brought a girl to meet the group before. Must be serious. Don't break his heart—he's one of the good ones."

Ten minutes later, we watched the game kick off. Daniel weaved through the opposition, his movements fluid and deliberate. He scored a try and punched the air, his eyes meeting mine as the ref awarded five points.

"Go get 'em, Daniel!" I shouted.

Jazz leaned over. "How long have you known him?"

"Just a few days. We met at a coffee shop. It was… an instant connection."

"Gosh, he's usually so shy. I've never seen him approach anyone like that." Jazz's eyes widened in surprise.

Warmth crept over me and I smiled. "Well, I must be lucky then. How long have you known him?"

"About four years, since he joined the rugby team. The only other girl he's brought here was his sister, Megan."

"What's she like?"

"Like Daniel—quiet but warm, always smiling. They're from Devon, I think."

I nodded, absorbing this new piece of the puzzle. "I don't know much about him yet. Were they born in the UK?"

"I believe so. Their parents came over from the West Indies in the 60s and settled in Devon."

Suddenly, a chant echoed through the crowd, cutting off our conversation. "HEEEAAAAVVVEEE!" Jazz joined in without hesitation, and I followed, laughing. I had no idea what we were shouting, but it didn't matter. Soon we were all giggling, throwing our voices into the air, "HEEEAAAAVVVEEE!" and then something about a "Garryowen!"

Before I knew it, halftime arrived. Daniel jogged over, flushed and sweaty, with Pete trailing behind.

"Enjoying it, Lu?" Daniel grinned as he took a swig of water.

"What's not to enjoy? Seeing a bunch of men prancing around in shorts."

Daniel raised an eyebrow. "So, not a rugby girl, then?"

With a thoughtful tap on my chin, "Umm, dominating the breakdown is crucial for the second half."

He let out a laugh. "Wow, a rugby expert now, are we?"

I shook my head, laughing softly. "I'd like to say I'm a quick learner, but really I found the phrase on my phone on the way here."

"Thank goodness for that, you almost had me fooled." He leaned in to kiss me, his lips brushing mine, sending warmth through my cheeks. As he pulled away, he pushed a piece of stray hair behind my ear. "Anyway, I'm back on." He jogged back to the field, turning briefly to wave. Sweat glistened on his forehead, dripping onto the grass beneath his boots.

The rest of the game drifted by in a haze. Uneasiness settled within me as the thoughts that had been troubling me since yesterday resurfaced. Daniel, selling drugs—it didn't fit. A PE teacher who made drug deals through Craigslist? Was it the thrill? The money? Debt? I needed answers.

The questions rattled around in my head until the final whistle blew, signalling the end of the match: St Peter's 29, St Jude's 17. The team erupted in cheers. Laughter and chatter filled the air, along with the pop of champagne corks and the spray of beer bottles being opened. My hands ached from all the high fives and clapping.

Showered and changed, the players pulled us into the clubhouse, where the Killers – *Human* blared from large speakers.

Daniel slid his arm around my waist as we entered. "Fancy a dance?"

I nodded, letting him lead me through the double doors. Inside buzzed with life. Trestle tables covered with sausage rolls, sandwiches, and crisps stretched out along the walls. The bar was a jumble of brass horseshoes, beer taps, and people queuing for their drinks.

But what caught my eye was the jukebox. A gleaming chrome monster of a thing, with a carousel that could hold up to 100 singles. It sat like a king in the corner, belting out tunes through big chrome speakers. Daniel grinned. "It's on free play today. Let's dance to The Killers, then we'll pick something else."

We made our way through the crowd, his arms around me, our bodies falling into rhythm. By the time we reached Pete and the others, we were moving to the beat, mouthing the lyrics. For the first time in ages, I let go. The questions about Daniel, the drugs, everything, faded. For now, I danced as carefree as a feather in the breeze.

As night crept in, the scent of barbecue filled the air, the grill outside doing a roaring trade. I stepped out to catch my breath, gazing up at the stars—a serene blanket over the chaos of the day. Beyond the grill, I watched Daniel in deep conversation with Pete, discussing rugby tactics. Stifling a yawn, Pete looked knackered.

I waved, smiling. "Come on, Daniel. Leave poor Pete to enjoy the rest of his evening with Rebecca."

"Alright, Lu." He stood, stretching. "Yours or mine?"

"Mine. I've got work in the morning."

Daniel groaned, rolling his eyes. "On a Sunday?"

"Yep, that's hospitality for you. I've got Wednesday off, though."

After collecting our coats and saying our goodbyes, we stepped out onto the street. The cold night air hit me, bringing with it the familiar smell of stale beer and sweat. Bodies lined the pavement, waiting for cabs or wandering towards the next pub.

A shout broke through the noise. "What you looking at, mate?"

I glanced over and saw a ginger lad in stag do antlers, his face bruised, blood streaking down his fancy dress outfit. He was slumped against some railings, chained up and hanging there like a broken puppet. Coins clinked in a hat beside him.

"Daniel, why's he shouting like that?"

Daniel's face paled. "That's Tim… He teaches history. I've got to help him."

Before I could react, Daniel sprinted towards Tim.

"Tim, it's Daniel! Let me get you down." Daniel crouched in front of him, his hands fumbling with the padlock.

A flicker of recognition crossed Tim's battered face; his eyes glassy beneath the blood. His breath came in ragged gasps. "You won't find the keys," he mumbled through gritted teeth. "They chucked them in the bin. My arms... they're coming out of their sockets. Hold me up, please."

Daniel's face tightened with strain as he tried to lift Tim's body, his voice urgent. "I need help! Someone, come and hold him! Lu, check the bin!"

My pulse quickened as I nodded, already running to the overflowing bin. From the corner of my eye, I saw two blokes rushing out of the clubhouse, sprinting towards Daniel. Without hesitation, I plunged my hands into the rubbish, pulling out scraps of litter that scattered across the pavement in a grimy cloud.

People walked by, glancing our way but not stopping. I could feel their judgment, and a coin rolled to my side with a mocking clink. Anger bubbled up inside me. "Can someone call 999? That man needs help!" My voice carried, cutting through the indifference around me.

A girl in a blue coat nudged her companion. "I'll call 999," she said, her eyes narrowing at his reluctance. "Go and help them, for God's sake."

The lad hesitated, his lips curling in a sneer as he took in the bin and the mess I was covered in—coffee-stains, bits of takeaway wrappers, and something I didn't want to think about clinging to my hands. He crouched down, muttering an awkward apology. "Sorry… about the coin."

I shot him a glance, half-exasperated. "It's alright, thanks for stepping up now."

We worked in silence for a moment before I straightened up. "You keep at the bin, I'll check the pavement." I moved away, scanning the ground with my phone's torch, kicking through discarded cans and soggy flyers.

The shrill of sirens grew louder, a promise of help finally on its way. I glanced over at Daniel, his face strained as he and his friends held Tim's body, keeping him propped up against the railings. My heart clenched at the sight, and I pushed harder, refusing to let failure be an option.

A shimmer caught the corner of my eye under a pile of leaves. Could it be? I bent down, fingers trembling as I parted them. There, glinting in the torchlight, were the keys.

"I've found them!" I yelled, stumbling over to Daniel and the others. "By the tree, not in the bin. Bloody liars."

With the keys in hand, Daniel swiftly undid the locks, and Tim slumped into their arms, free at last. With care, they lowered him to the ground, and a collective cheer erupted from the small group of us. Relief swept over me as I knelt to help the girl in the blue coat and her friend put the rubbish back in the bin.

By the time the police and ambulance arrived, Tim's face had paled with the cold, his body trembling with hypothermia and exhaustion. They wrapped him in a Myler blanket and loaded him into the ambulance, the flashing lights casting long shadows against the railings where he'd been trapped.

Before the ambulance drove off, Daniel managed to coax the names of the culprits from Tim—two sixth-form students he'd held in detention for plagiarising essays a few weeks back. Admiration swelled in me as Daniel filled me in.

"Well, you're brilliant, though I'm hardly surprised," he said, a grin forming as he looked over at Tim.

"Do you know him well? I can't believe he's a teacher. He doesn't look the part," I said, kicking at a pile of leaves, trying to shake off the unease growing inside me.

"Doesn't he? What about me? Do I fit the bill?"

I hesitated, meeting Daniel's gaze. "No… not really. But then again, you don't exactly scream 'drug dealer,' either."

He chuckled, though his eyes shifted uneasily checking the police were out of earshot. "Oh? Looking to buy more?"

"Not today," I said lightly, "but maybe in a few days."

Relief flickered across his face, but he couldn't help fidgeting, picking at imaginary lint on his jumper in the dim light. I squeezed his hand, trying to ground him. "If we're heading back to mine, I need the truth."

"Not here." The turn of his head took in the group of people who lingered, heatedly discussing 'the youth of today.' "Let's walk back to yours. I'll explain as we go."

The walk would only take half an hour. "Okay." I slipped my hand into his and we set off. For once the night sky portrayed a cloudless blue straight from a Van Gogh painting, leaving the street lights to pale in its glow. The graffiti covered buildings displayed fabulous artistry that detracted from the dirt and grime of Dalston's streets.

Caught up in the colours of a painted carnival, I jumped when he began to share with me.

"Two years ago, my sister got tangled up with a local drugs gang in Devon. She started small—weed, then onto harder stuff. Cannabis, mainly."

"Bloody hell, Dan. Sorry to hear that."

"It tore our family apart." His voice cracked, and I tightened my grip on his hand. "She was hooked, Lu. Desperate for her next hit. You understand where this goes, right?"

"I think so." I tried to convey with my tone that I was there for him.

"They threatened to expose her, sent me videos, photos… and samples. Said I had to clear her debt or they'd make it worse."

The seriousness of his words hit me, but I stayed quiet, gently squeezing his hand to urge him on. His body trembled as the memories overtook him.

"I tried to buy her out—offered to pay the whole amount. But they didn't want money, they wanted control."

"Megan must have been terrified." I could imagine the horror of it.

He dropped his head forward, lost in his pain. "We forced her into rehab. Two months—she hated us for it, but it worked. She's clean now, living somewhere new, trying to rebuild."

"I'd like to meet her, if that's okay with you?"

"Sure. She visits every month."

Silence fell between us, a welcome respite after the flood of revelations. We continued walking towards my place. It never ceased to surprise me how busy the streets stayed, day and night. The hum of traffic always there.

As we neared my flat, I broke the quiet. "So… what happened to the gang?"

Daniel exhaled deeply, eyes locking with mine. "They make me sell for them—weed, coke, whatever they want. That's how we ended up meeting at the coffee shop. Craigslist was their idea."

I couldn't contain the shiver that coursed through me. "How much longer do you have to do this?"

"Another year."

"And then it's over?" My heart twisted, caught between the growing affection I had for Daniel and the reality of his situation—one I should run a million miles from, but knew I wouldn't.

He nodded, but the despair in his eyes told me he wasn't sure. I wanted to believe the good guy could win for once. My mind whirled, already forming a plan, but I forced myself to let it go. For now.

Unlocking the door, I led Daniel up to my flat, where Ted—the bedraggled stuffed bear—sat slumped in his usual spot. Daniel's gaze fell on him, concern lining his face.

"God, Ted's had a rough night. Poor thing looks like he's taken a beating."

"Next door's cat." I cringed at the easy way the lie flew from my mouth. "Got in and attacked him. I'll patch him up after work tomorrow."

Daniel pulled me into his arms. "Let me take him. I'll get him properly fixed for you."

I let out a soft laugh, brushing aside my guilt. "Sure, thanks."

As his lips found mine, Ted and all the thoughts about the drugs disappeared. Our clothes slid to the floor in a lust-filled frenzy as we undressed each other. Hungry for confirmation of acceptance, needing each other, and willing to temporarily forget the problems of the world in our desire for connection.

*****

The next morning, I slipped out quietly, leaving Daniel sleeping soundly in bed, clutching the spare key. I told myself I couldn't walk away from him now. Whatever lay ahead, I wasn't ready to give up on the best thing that had ever happened to me.

Besides, all night this crazy, crazy idea had been building.

Chapter 5

Lucy—Paracosm

AS I SAT at my desk, my thoughts raced. Names flickered across my mind—friends, contacts. It wouldn't take much to tap into that circle. Discretion would be key, but I could handle it. And with only a year left for Daniel, he'd be free soon enough.

I shot off the first text: I've had an idea to help you. I could work with you and sell to people I know we can trust. I'd need regular supplies and good prices.

Daniel's reply came back quickly: My god, you're amazing. But are you sure? It's just a year, you could be putting yourself in danger. For me, it's perfect. I can forget Craigslist and focus on supplying. And anything you want is free, obviously.

I typed: I know what I'm doing, and I believe in you. Forget about listing. And thanks for the freebies. You could've so easily been caught and lost your job. I hit send before I had a chance to second-guess.

Daniel: I'll contact them now. I have Ted. Thanks, you're a sweetheart xx

My fingers hovered over the screen before typing: Ted will be pleased to finally get his fix! xx

The first week flew by, a blur of activity and new faces. It was shocking how fast word spread. Orders came in left, right, and centre. And no one batted an eyelid. As long as I stayed under the radar, it was smooth sailing. The bum bag made it easy, the little packets passing unnoticed—sugar substitutes for a sweeter kind of high.

Daniel started sporting more gold than before, but I had to admit, it suited him. The transformation was subtle but undeniable. He was happier, lighter, and our nights…well, they had an extra edge, fuelled by our little recreational habits. The high made everything sharper, clearer, even the blurry lines of what we were doing.

Moving in together felt like the next natural step. The penthouse at Canary Wharf was a far cry from the grim loft conversion flat in Dalston. We'd traded the seedy backstreets for sleek city views, and I couldn't help but feel like we were on the verge of something bigger.

*****

Three months of living in the fast lane passed in a flash. We'd slotted together so naturally. Selling drugs became second nature and nothing to worry about.

A big day for me arrived when my parents came to see the new place, eager to meet Daniel. As soon as they stepped in, Dad's eyes swept over the new curtains, the fresh furniture, the roll of cash casually left on the counter.

"What a fabulous place. What does Daniel do?" Dad's eyes lingered on a particularly large wad of notes.

"He's a PE teacher at a school nearby," I said, my voice steady, though my heart thudded. I saw the way he took in the luxury that didn't quite match the salary of a teacher.

His eyes darted to my teddy. "Ted's had a bit of a makeover, hasn't he?"

"Daniel did that for me. He's so thoughtful." I smiled, my chest swelling with pride.

Mum, her voice softer, "You're still working at The A1-Chemist, right?" She couldn't quite hide the tremor in her words.

"Yes, Mum, we're fine. Honestly. What is it with you two? You're always looking for problems where there aren't any." I can't help a tiny cringe saying that after all they'd done for me.

"We're not." Dad shared a look with Mum. "We just worry about you."

Their smiles were forced, and I knew what they were thinking.

The front door clicked, and I jumped up, rushing to greet Daniel. "Here he is—the love of my life." I placed his slippers down like it was a ritual.

"No need for that today, Lu." Daniel stepped inside, flashing his usual wide grin.

My parents exchanged a glance, their expressions stiffening as they eyed his gold chains, designer joggers, and fresh kicks. They didn't say anything, but their silent judgment irritated me.

Luckily, Daniel remained oblivious. "Patrick, Nancy! Or should I call you Mum and Dad?" With a cheeky smile, he held out his hand to my father.

Dad's voice was polite but clipped; the tone I always thought of as his 'no-nonsense' mode. "Great to meet you, Daniel. Just call us Patrick and Nancy."

Mum tried to keep it light. "Nice place you've got here."

"We moved in a few months back. Perfect for the future." Daniel winked at me, making me blush.

Mum didn't miss it, shooting me an astute beam. "So, it's serious between you two?"

Daniel and I just grinned like school kids.

Dad handed over a bottle of champagne. "Well, let's celebrate, shall we?"

Two bottles later, we were all sitting on the terrace, laughter mixing with the city noise.

The warmth of the champagne loosened everyone up, but Dad couldn't resist a dig with one arched eyebrow. "This place must cost a fortune."

Daniel chuckled. "Hard work pays off, Patrick. As you know."

I tried to cut the conversation before it went where I didn't want it to go, "Dad, enough!"

Mum swooped in, steering us away from money. "So, Daniel, tell us about your job, your hobbies?"

"I'm a PE teacher at St Peter's. I love it. And I play for a rugby team, too. Lu's seen me in action."

I smiled into Daniel's mesmerizing eyes, remembering our second date. "Yeah, it was quite a show. There's something about a man in shorts."

Mum shifted uncomfortably, and Dad cleared his throat, but inside I was dancing. *Who couldn't love Daniel?*

Casual, appearing relaxed, Dad addressed Daniel. "You look fit, do you work out?"

Daniel's head swelled before my eyes and I shook my head with a grin. *Men and praise!*

"I go three times a week before work. It keeps me in top form for rugby," he grinned at me, "and other things."

"Do you think you could give me some tips?"

"Sure, though I don't know when we'll have time to fit it in this weekend."

I raised an eyebrow and stared at Dad's pot belly. *Since when are you into fitness?*

Dad turned to me. "You'll have to come up to ours, and Daniel can take me to the gym. I've always wanted to join, isn't that so, Nancy?"

Mum nods. "Yes, he has, and it would be good for me and Lucy to try out the spa facilities too."

"Now you're talking Mum. We'll go, won't we, Daniel?"

"Of course," Daniel replied smoothly. "I'd love to see the family home. Maybe then I can call you Mum and Dad?"

Dad chuckled. "Let's see how it goes."

The evening ended with fish and chips, champagne, and a lot of laughter. As we sat around the table, I squeezed Daniel's hand under the table. Safety and love wrapped around me like a warm embrace. My happiness had spilled over to Mum and Dad who were both at ease and happy. Today had gone better than I could've imagined.

*****

The first sign something was wrong came two weeks later. Daniel stumbled through the door, his face swollen, black eyes glaring through smears of dried blood, cradling his arm like it might shatter.

The cup in my hand slipped, smashing against the floor as hot coffee splashed down my leg. "Shit, I've spilt my coffee. It's boiling." My voice shook as I stared at the red, angry skin.

"Cold water. Ten minutes. Go!"

Daniel's voice cut through my panic and I ran to the bathroom, adrenaline pumping, limbs trembling. With one leg in the bath, I kept it under the stream, counting every agonising second. By the time I limped back, a raw, red patch covered my skin, stinging with each step.

Daniel lay sprawled out on the sofa, blood still seeping through his clothes. "You'll be fine."

I stared at him, hands hovering, not knowing whether to scream or cry. The words came out in a hiss. "What the hell happened to you?"

"Nothing, Lu. Walked into a tree." His voice was strained, flat, and he avoided my eyes.

A bitter laugh escaped me. "No tree did that. You're a mess. Your arm looks broken." I lowered myself next to him and reached up to touch his face, the bruises throbbed beneath the tips of my fingers. "We'll get you fixed up, and then you're telling me the truth. No more lies."

He didn't argue. He kept his eyes on the floor as I helped him into his jacket.

Wrapping it around him, a surge of warmth ran through me; I was his protector now, responsible for patching him up. With tenderness and mock bossiness, "A&E it is then."

I could hardly hear his answer. "Whatever." His body trembled as I guided him to the door.

The hospital was grim at night, all harsh lights and cold air. COVID rules meant I had to wait outside, alone on a bench in the dark. Time dragged, and I kept checking my phone; I'd have to call in sick for my late shift soon.

Four hours later, he emerged, slumped in a wheelchair with his arm in a plaster cast resting in a sling, but still managing a lopsided grin.

I smiled back, relief washing over me. For the briefest moment, it felt like we were invincible, the perfect couple, untouchable.

The next morning, with Daniel too ill to drag himself to work, I curled up beside him. The air was heavy, thick with unspoken words. I took a deep breath and tried to keep my voice as soft as possible, "Are you going to tell me what really happened? No sugar-coating, please."

He squeezed my hands, his eyes dull, all their usual sparkle gone. "It was Samuel Samson and his lot. He said we're dealing on his patch. We owe him twenty grand. Yesterday was…a warning."

My heart dropped. "A warning? He's a bloody animal, Daniel. You're lucky you weren't killed."

Daniel looked away; his voice low. "We've got to stop. Both of us. Or we're dead meat."

My skin prickled, hairs standing on end. "Would it really come to that?"

"Yes, Lu. This isn't a joke. He's in the big leagues, and we're stepping on his toes."

I took a deep breath, trying to process. "How have you managed all this time? You've been dealing for years, haven't you?"

"I stayed small. Under the radar. But now...with you involved, we've built something bigger. Too big."

I frowned, frustration bubbling up. "So why are we always skint then? Why are we always only scraping by?"

Daniel gave me a weary smile, full of bitterness. "Expensive tastes, Lu. And half the profit goes to the Devon gang."

"We're screwed if we can't sell here." The words hung heavy between us.

He nodded, defeated.

"How long have you got left with the Devon gang?"

"Eight months."

My eyes narrowed. "Those videos must have something terrible on them. Your sister should've paid them off by now, shouldn't she?"

Warning bells. This wasn't over. Not even close. A veil lifted and I understood that there was still something going on I didn't know about. *What aren't you telling me?* Subconsciously, I pushed the thought aside because more than anything I wanted this relationship to work.

*****

Six weeks later, we drove through the tall, black iron gates, following the winding tree-lined driveway that led to my family home. The sight of Mum and Dad waiting at the front door, Rufus wagging his tail excitedly beside them, made something inside me settle.

"Lovely place, Lu," Daniel said, mouth agape. "Must've been something growing up here." His eyes sparkled with a hint of greed.

I laughed, nudging him playfully. "Put your tongue back in. We're almost there."

He handed me a small bag, and I squeezed his hand, trying to steady the swirl of emotions building inside me. "It'll go fine," Daniel reassured me.

"I know, but they've had a hard time in the past. I don't want to add to it."

As I ran into their arms, a sense of calm washed over me. Home. Safe. They, on the other hand, unwittingly welcomed a brewing storm.

Daniel had gone all out, looking sharp in his burgundy joggers, beige top, and chunky gold necklace. He'd added a nose ring, and slicked back his gorgeous long afro into a neat ponytail. I had to admit, he looked striking, and he'd got me in on the act too.

Dressed in white joggers, a matching top, and my favourite gold heart necklace, I'd found a new style that suited me and gave me a sense of belonging. The latest Prada, plain black baseball cap covering my blonde bob added the final touch.

Rufus bounded up, a stick clamped in his mouth, tail wagging furiously. He dropped it at my feet and sat back, waiting, bright-eyed. I teased him, bending down then standing up again, just like I used to when I was a kid. When I launched the stick across the garden, narrowly missing the pond, Rufus darted off, bounding along on old legs with the joy of a pup.

He returned panting, the stick soggy and slimy. This time, Daniel threw it behind him, watching Rufus's head tilt in confusion before he spotted it on the far side of the garden. With a playful hop and skip, Rufus disappeared into the brambles, emerging covered in blackberry thorns. Daniel and I doubled over in laughter as Rufus triumphantly dropped the stick onto Daniel's pristine trainers.

Patting Rufus's head, Daniel grinned. "Oh, mate, what are we going to do with you?"

He tossed the stick again as Mum appeared in the doorway. "Let's go inside before Rufus demands all your attention."

We went into the hallway; its wide, tiled floors gleaming. Daniel's gaze drifted to the family photos lining the walls. "Is that you, Lu? The skinny Goth with the red cardigan?"

I chuckled, embarrassed. "Yeah, that was my Goth phase. Real looker, right?"

Daniel wrapped his arm around me. "Cute, I'd say. And in a band too? Is there no end to your talents?"

I smiled shyly. "I was the lead singer. We did a lot of gigs."

"Well, watch out, Adele," Daniel quipped, his voice playful but proud.

As we made our way into the kitchen, a wave of nostalgia hit me. Mum had laid out a feast, colourful platters of food that covered every craving. We dived in, laughter and chatter filling the room, a sound that had been missing for far too long.

Later, stuffed and content, I collapsed onto the navy-blue sofa, my head resting in Daniel's lap. "This is the life."

Mum smiled warmly. "You always liked to snuggle up on the sofa. Some things never change."

I laughed. "Oh, but we have a white leather sofa now, Mum. Not quite the same." I shifted, wincing at the thought of our too-modern apartment. "Not exactly snuggling material."

Daniel put his hands out and shrugged. "Hey, it's got clean lines. Very contemporary."

"See what I'm up against?"

Dad chimed in with a grin, posing in front of us with a side-profile. "Let's forget the gym today, eh?"

"Ugh, Dad, gross!" I reached over and gave his belly a playful pat.

Mum chuckled at him. "He's seeing how big it'll grow."

Dad laughed, but his voice softened. "It's good to see you both."

"And Rufus likes you, Daniel. He doesn't warm to strangers easily. Remember Jordan?" Both Mum's eyebrows shot up her forehead.

I sighed, tipping my head back. "Not that story again."

Daniel looked intrigued. "I need to hear this."

Mum giggled, tears forming in her eyes. "Oh, Rufus took one sniff at Jordan and went straight for his leg. Took a chunk out of him!"

More laughter erupted, even Rufus, clueless as he chased his tail, seemed to join in. Mum scolded him, and with his tail between his legs, he slinked out of the room belly almost to the floor, only to return moments later, collapsing in a heap beside me.

Warmth washed over me as I stroked Rufus's head. For the first time in ages, everything felt... possible. Eager to keep the mood light I offered, "Latte, anyone?"

Dad raised a hand. "Irish coffee for me. Make it strong."

Daniel grinned. "I'll take one of those too."

Mum and I linked arms and made our way to the kitchen and after finding the coffee pods and putting water in the

Nespresso, we sat down, taking in the brightly coloured flowers adorning the fields in the distance.

"I love this place, Mum, it's great to be home at last. It's been too long." Breathing deeply, I soak in the familiar.

Mum's eyes took on a sharp edge. "I can always tell when something's up. What's wrong?"

I hesitated. "Daniel... he got jumped by a gang six weeks ago. They broke his arm; he only had the cast removed last week."

Mum's face paled. "Why didn't you tell us?"

I shrugged, trying to brush it off. "He's fine now. It was... rough, but we're managing though he's been off work since it happened."

Mum wiped away a tear and pulled me close. "If you ever need anything, you know we're here. You can wrap your dad around your little finger. Tell me, is that why you've started biting the skin around your nails again?"

Putting my hands behind my back I went bright red. "I didn't think you'd notice, Mum."

"I notice everything, I thought you'd realised that by now?"

Tears pricked my eyes. "I'm scared, Mum. London's getting dangerous, and Daniel's too trusting. We both are."

"Then come home. Stay with us."

I shook my head. "What about you and Dad? Are you okay?"

Mum gave me a reassuring smile. "We're better. No more boozing, no more... mess. He's reinstated Alan and Mark at the site. Things are looking up."

Relief flooded me. "I was so scared I'd failed you both. I never wanted to come from a broken home… or be the cause of it."

Mum hugged me tighter. "You could never fail us."

"Let's make this coffee then and bring it to the boys. So glad you'll be coming home. Is this what Daniel wants though?"

"Yes Mum, we've talked about moving out of London, but never imagined in our wildest dreams that we might be able to come here."

As we made our way back to the front room with coffee and cake, my heart raced. Daniel caught my eye, his gaze steady. This was it. Time to face whatever came next.

Mum glowed like the cat that got the cream and it wasn't lost on Dad.

"What have you two been cooking up?" Dad nudged Daniel's shoulder. "They're up to something, I can always tell."

Daniel smiled, his eyes searching mine. "Don't know what that could be," he said, but the way he squeezed my hand said otherwise. As I bent down, he whispered, "Clever girl."

We spent a couple of hours catching up, followed by working together in the kitchen to make sandwiches and fresh lemonade. After the light lunch, Mum and Dad said they needed to work off the calories and left us to watch a movie.

We kept glancing at the clock. By five, nothing had been said, and the jitters set in. Every minute stretched like an eternity, each tick of the grandfather clock in the hallway growing louder in my ears.

We were running out of time to set up a new circle of clients so we'd have the money to start repaying the debt. The 'warning' Daniel had received would soon turn into something worse if we didn't cough up the money. Both of us knew Lapworth was perfect—remote enough to hide and keep things quiet, yet close enough to deal from.

Outside, Mum and Dad were "deadheading the roses," or so they claimed. But seeing them with their heads close together, hands idle, I knew they were up to something entirely different.

"I can't take this, Daniel. I have to talk to them," I said, the words spilling out in a rush.

"Give it a minute. Why don't we take some tea and biscuits down to the workers?" He gave me that sideways smile, the one that usually worked.

I grabbed onto the distraction like a lifeline. "Great idea."

The clatter of cups and the high-pitched whistle of the kettle filled the kitchen. Daniel joined me, fetching the biscuit tin and prepping the tray, conspiracy swirling between us.

Picking up the tray, Daniel locked eyes with me. "This is it."

We laughed as we carried the tray outside, tossing Rufus's ball along the way. He bounded after it, his tongue lolling, tail wagging madly. When he dropped the ball at Daniel's feet, I smiled. "Well, he likes you. That's a good start."

Daniel lobbed the ball again, this time sending it sailing over the garden wall.

I froze as the sound of shattering glass cut through the air, followed by heavy footsteps and a cry of dismay. "Oh no…" Vince, our next-door neighbour, had a greenhouse full of prize tomatoes.

From the other side of the wall, we heard Vince shout, "Who broke the glass?"

"It was me and Daniel, Uncle Vince. I'm so sorry."

He sounded gruff but not truly angry. "Right, Miss Lucy. I didn't know you were back."

We heard more glass breaking and pots clattering, the sound of frustration. Dad sprinted to the wall, with Mum, Daniel, and me following behind.

Vince's voice echoed over the wall. "Harvest festival's next week. Those were my best tomatoes. I'll never win the 'Best in Class' now."

Dad turned to us, his lips twitching. "Vince's well-known for his veggies. He even judges some categories."

I hunched my shoulders and pulled a comical face at Daniel before raising my voice. "Uncle Vince, it's me, Lucy. I swear it won't happen again."

"Clumsy as ever, I see! No change there." Vince's tone softened, and I knew he wasn't upset.

Daniel stepped in. "Sorry, Vince, it's my fault. I threw the ball for Rufus. I'm Lucy's boyfriend; we're here for a few days. I'm a rugby player; guess my throw is stronger than I thought."

On the other side of the fence, Vince chuckled. "Oh, so it's you I have to blame?"

"Or Rufus. He should've caught the ball," Daniel quipped, and laughter rippled through the garden.

Dad grinned, amused, "Well, Daniel, looks like you'll be staying a while to fix Vince's greenhouse."

Daniel's eyes sparkled. "Thanks, Patrick." He cupped his hands over his mouth and shouted over the wall, "I'll make sure to do a proper job, Vince."

Dad's grin widened. "You can start calling me 'Dad,' now that you're sticking around."

A jolt of joy went through me as Dad's gaze softened. "Lucy, you can put that tray down now. The way you're bouncing around, there's more tea in the saucers than in the cups."

My hands shook as I set the tray on the table. Vince's laughter echoed from the other side of the wall. "She's back, alright!"

"Only for a few weeks," Mum chimed in, but the warmth in her voice made it sound like forever.

"Welcome to the family, Daniel." Her wide and approving smile warmed my heart.

Daniel came back with a tongue-in-cheek response that made me blush. "Thanks, Mum! It's got a nice ring to it."

Mum gave me a thumbs-up, her grin contagious. I glanced down at my feet, biting my lip at the big step just taken. Daniel had crossed a line today, and for better or worse, there was no going back.

*****

The next day, I rang in sick, knowing there'd be no chance of asking for a reference anytime soon. They'd figure out soon enough that I'd left them high and dry. My clients would be furious—I could only hope they wouldn't show up at work and make a scene. If they dug too deep, my under-the-table dealings would be exposed, and that would be a whole new level of disaster.

Daniel was still off work, so aside from the rugby lads and his friends, no one would notice right away. He said he had to call his sister. When she picked up, she cried and cursed, but she knew there was nothing she could do. This mess was on her, anyway. I offered to speak to her, to reassure her that we'd make good on our obligations to the Devon gang. But Daniel shot me a look that stopped me cold.

His voice was firm when he spoke. "Even my family can't know where we're headed, not with the kind of pressure they could put on us."

He promised to reach out to the gang in a few days, once things had settled, to sort out new supplies.

Chapter 6

Lucy—Who is the Biggest Liar?

AS I DROVE toward Lapworth village centre to go to work, a rush of excitement swelled inside me, my heart racing with the anticipation of returning to the rolling hills of Warwickshire. This was it—our fresh start. Mum and Dad had opened their home to us, laughing they'd promised that Rufus would be on his best behaviour, which felt like a minor miracle in itself.

The owners of Soogun, a trendy spot in Dickens Heath, offered me a job. By day, it was all about coffee for the ladies who lunched, and by night, it transformed into a buzzing place for the younger crowd. While mixology was my preference, I'd soon become pretty good at serving up the lattes and cappuccinos. The owners didn't ask for a reference—they knew my parents and had somehow heard of my past. They still gave me the job, which was both kind and somewhat reckless.

Daniel, still too unwell for full-time work, had managed to secure a part-time maternity cover position teaching PE at a nearby school. Though the younger students weren't his usual preference, the flexibility of the job left him plenty of time for his "side projects."

This time, we shifted our sales to Facebook Marketplace and the streets, targeting posh sixth-formers hanging around Morrisons in Knowle after school. The kids weren't users themselves, but they had no problem spending their parents' money to dabble in something lucrative. Meanwhile, my daytime clientele at Soogun—bored housewives with deep pockets—became a steady source of income for us. It was easy to win their trust, easier still to sell them what they needed to numb the monotony of their lives.

"We've got some great reviews coming in, Lucy. You're a real asset, and we're already looking at bumping up your pay," my manager, Audrey, told me one afternoon.

"That's brilliant news, thank you! Mum and Dad will be delighted. Daniel and I might be able to get our own place sooner than we thought."

Life in Warwickshire was shaping up better than we'd hoped. Daniel couldn't stop grinning—our phones didn't stop ringing, and for once, we weren't stepping on anyone else's toes.

Coming up behind me, Daniel wrapped his arms around my waist and nuzzled his nose on my neck. "Let's go out tonight, Lu, to celebrate. How about a proper date night?"

I smiled, a rare contentment washing over me. "I'm in. Let's make it just us two. I've got a new Basque I want to wear… we might want to get home in a hurry!"

"Is it the Fourth of July or something?" Daniel teased.

I laughed. "No, silly, I just want to show you how happy I am."

"Umm, I like the sound of that. Alright then, how about we swing by Solihull and do some window shopping?"

I raised an eyebrow. "No more gold for you. Mum's already got her eye on half your wardrobe!"

He let go of me and swung me around to face him. He tapped my nose with his finger. "Fine, fine, but maybe I'll buy you something instead. How about a ring… one with sapphires and diamonds?"

I blinked, caught off guard. "Wait—are you serious? Is this your way of asking?"

His grin couldn't have been wider. "Sure is, and once we're done, we can bring some fizz home for Mum and Dad."

I bounced on my toes with excitement. "I can't believe this. Of course I'll say yes!" I ruffled his hair, a smile plastered on my face. "I love it when you call them Mum and Dad."

Later that night, Daniel dropped to one knee, the ring shining like a beacon in his hand. His earnest face locked onto mine, and a spark passed between us. The silence crackled. Behind her hand, a woman nearby said, "She has to say yes. They're stunning together, absolutely magnetic."

A waiter motioned for her to lower her voice, but cameras flashed, blinding us in bursts of light. My heart raced; my mind unable to process the moment. I'd waited for this my whole life. "Yes," I said, my voice trembling with disbelief. "Of course I'll marry you."

The restaurant fell silent around us. The candlelight caught the diamond as Daniel slid the ring onto my finger, and suddenly the room erupted in applause, a Champagne cork popped to our left. We were the centre of attention, and for once, I didn't mind.

When I held it up, the diamond sparkled so brightly it could have guided planes through the fog. "I love you!" The rush of emotion made it almost impossible to hear myself.

As the 'Lapworth Trio' came over to serenade us with *The Greatest Love of All,* I shrank in my seat, laughing nervously. "Did you arrange this?"

Daniel shook his head. "Nope. That was your Dad's doing. Had to ask for your hand properly, didn't I?"

"Typical Dad," I said fondly.

For the first time in ages, I felt completely secure. But beneath the surface, my mood shifted. A sudden chill crept over me, tightening my grip on the table.

Daniel picked up on my mood right away. "You alright, Lu?"

I tried to brush it off, but I shivered. "Someone... walked over my grave."

The moment passed, and I shook it off, pretending it hadn't happened. We left the restaurant, hand in hand, but I couldn't shake the foreboding that something terrible loomed ahead of us.

Later, in the taxi home, the wind rattled through the trees, leaves swirling in the moon's pale light. The house came into view, and I shivered. The garden, usually bright and inviting full of fairy lights and pathway guides, lay in darkness. The birch trees swayed unnaturally, the wind sweeping up leaves and hurling them across the lawn. Anxiety came like the Grim Reaper. "Daniel, you did ask Dad's permission to marry me, didn't you?"

Daniel wagged his finger, but with less certainty than usual. "Course I did, love. Something tells me your mum knows too."

"She might." I tugged at his hand to get him to stop walking. We'd been dropped off by the back gate to save time for the taxi driver.

Colour drained from my face as I looked up at him. "Where are they?"

"They're probably inside, waiting for us."

I shook my head. "Something's not right." Then I saw it—a dark mound by the back door. My hands flew to my mouth to stop a scream. Rufus! His blood-soaked fur was matted, a stick lodged in his mouth.

I collapsed in tears, my body shaking uncontrollably. "Who did this?"

Daniel crouched down beside me, his voice soft and gentle. "It must have been quick. By the looks of it, he didn't suffer."

We circled the house, peering through the window into the lounge. Mum and Dad were gagged and bound together, while three men stood behind them, guns in hand arguing between themselves, balaclavas over their heads.

"I'm going to call the police."

"No, Lu, there's no time. Plus, I think I recognise them."

We crept back around to the rear of the house. "Who are they, and how can you recognize them when their faces are covered?"

"I'd know them anywhere. The tall one is Samuel Sampson and the other two are his sidekicks." His breath hitched. "They've found me."

"But why follow us here?"

"Because of the money I owe them."

"How much?"

"Three million in lost revenue."

I froze. "Three million? What the—! My parents are inside. I can't lose them! I'm calling the police."

"We can't involve them yet. Trust me" His voice had an edge of panic. He pulled out a gun from his jacket. I recoiled, the pieces finally clicking together.

The gold, the fancy lifestyle, the lies, and the mysterious sister I could never meet—it all came crashing down. I didn't know who the man in front of me was. He certainly wasn't the 'caring brother' he pretended to be.

I'd never seen a photograph of his parents or anything from his past. He'd said he liked 'clean-lines' but in a flash I understood the lack of personal items had nothing to do with Feng Shui and everything to do with his hidden persona. He was nothing more than a drug dealer and I'd been bamboozled into his lying sob story.

As we slipped into the house, the sound of threats filtered through the hallway. Glass shattered followed by a spate of curses.

Fury boiling inside me. The terror of Rufus's body, of Mum and Dad gagged and bound—it all erupted.

Without a second thought, I shoved Daniel into the walk-in freezer, the door slamming shut just as a deafening gunshot reverberated through the house. Panic surged as the sound rattled my bones. Panic fuelled me and I burst into the lounge, my heart hammering so hard I thought I was dying.

Still bound, Mum and Dad's eyes widened with fear. The three men turned to face me, their eyes shifting from surprise to rage.

"What the hell is going on?" one of them barked, his hand tightening around the grip of his weapon. "Where's Steve? Tell me now or I'll put a bullet in one of them."

"Steve? You mean Daniel? He's locked in the freezer." Urgency propelled me forward to my parents. I positioned myself in front of them, desperate to shield them from the awfulness I'd brought into their lives.

The tall one leaned against the wall, a sinister smirk playing on his lips. "I understand now why they call you Solihull girls 'Posh Totty,'" he sneered, eyes glinting with malice as he checked me out. "Thirty seconds to tell me before I put a bullet in your mother's head."

Sweat beaded on my forehead. A prickling sensation ran up my spine.

Bravado came out of the blue. "Take him—whoever he is—but don't hurt my parents!" My voice trembled with a mix of fear and defiance. The horror on Mum and Dad's faces pierced through me, twisting my gut. *God, what have I done?*

Samuel pushed himself off the wall. "Let's get our guy and go."

"Congrats on the engagement, by the way," one of the other two chuckled, the laughter echoing as he walked into the hallway, sending chills down my spine.

In a surge of fury, I snatched a plate from the table and flung it at them, the china shattering against the wall with a violent crash, splintering the glass of Mum's favourite cabinet into a thousand gleaming shards.

Samuel reappeared in the doorway; gun pointed straight at me. He snorted. "Crackhead."

We heard the freezer door swing open, then the sickening sound of Daniel being dragged out, pleading, his voice full of terror.

I collapsed next to Mum and Dad, fumbling with the knots on their bindings. As we clung to each other, Dad placed a finger on my lips.

"No more," he said, his tone sharp but trembling. "At least he's out of our lives now."

From outside, Daniel's desperate cries cut through the silence, followed by a dull thud. Then nothing.

"They're gone." Dad's face paled.

Mum placed a hand on his arm. "Should we call the police?"

"We've been through enough tonight. He got what he deserved."

Mum turned to me, her voice soft. "Are you alright, Darling?"

I couldn't bring myself to look at her. "I loved him, you know… but we did awful things together." Guilt gnawed at my insides. "I'll make it right. Do you want me to leave?"

Dad put his arm around me. "No, you stay. We're family. We'll figure this out. You know, on the surface, he came off as a good man—charming, easy to like—but underneath, there lurked something darker. He dealt drugs, lied without a second thought, yet his charisma pulled people in… even me."

Oddly, I sensed Dad knew more than he revealed, as though his rambling disguised what he wasn't saying. What struck me most, beyond the unspoken secrets, was the reassurance that I hadn't been the only one deceived.

Mum was already thinking ahead. "You can go to The Hedgeway. Get clean. We'll help you."

"Rufus is dead," I whimpered, breaking down again. "He's outside…"

"Enough!" Mum pulled me into a tight embrace. "Don't let that swine win. You're stronger than that." But as Mum held me, she sobbed with me, shock and the loss of Rufus as hard on her as it was me.

Her comfort did sooth me but inside I knew I was broken. *Why am I drawn to men like Daniel?*

"An hour ago, I was engaged." The absurdity of it all hit me and I dashed to the loo, sick with disgust.

When I returned, calm had settled back over the house. The china was being cleared, the room tidied. Mum looked up from sweeping the broken pieces. "Tea or something stronger?"

Dad sank into his chair. "Brandy."

I picked up a shard of glass. "Me too."

Rufus's absence hit me again. "What about Rufus? We can't leave him outside like that."

Dad sighed. "I'll ask Vince to come around tomorrow; he can take him to the vet for us. For now, we'll only use the front door."

"But he was my dog..."

Mum placed a hand on my arm. "What would you like to do?"

I paused, fighting back tears. "Could we bury him in the garden with a plaque? Something to remember him by."

Mum and Dad nodded, and a quick phone call later, Vince arrived. They carried Rufus away, and as the door closed behind them not able to watch as they buried him. Losing Daniel and Rufus on the same night, opened a gaping cavern in my heart, I'd lost a piece of myself I was sure I'd never get back.

I didn't know who I was anymore. There was this version of me—cool, confident, charming—always pulling off the perfect act in front of everyone. Then there was this... darker side, a part of me that felt like a fraud, like everything always unravelled around me, and I was powerless to stop it. Daniel played his role, sure, but it was me—I was the one who let it happen, who chose him and stayed despite the drugs.

What does that make me? I slipped the diamond ring off my finger and twirled it around. *Had it meant anything, did I mean anything?* Deep down, I knew I was no better than him. We were two sides of the same coin—both of us pretending, manipulating, covering up the rot underneath. I wasn't the victim here, was I? I was complicit. That's what scared me the most.

I could have walked away a hundred times, but I didn't. I thrived in the shadows, pretending that the highs justified the lows. Maybe I was too far gone. Maybe Daniel didn't corrupt me—maybe I was like this all along.

That night, sleep was impossible. By morning, the police were involved, and the truth laid bare.

Dad's private investigator had been following Daniel for months. He knew everything—the drugs, the deals. It had been Dad who tipped off Samuel Sampson.

Could I forgive him?

I wasn't sure.

Chapter 7

Nancy—and the Greatest Gift

THE FIRST TIME I held Lucy in my arms was the best day of my life. Unmarried, living in a mother-and-baby shelter wasn't the future I'd pictured for her, but I did the best I could. My strict Catholic parents had thrown me out when I got pregnant, so there I was, reliant on the state. I told people the father had run off to London the moment he heard about the baby, leaving me to fend for us both. The lie I repeated so often, took root until I believed it myself—the truth too abhorrent to remember.

I promised myself that I'd fight for Lucy, that I'd turn things around. Somehow, she would succeed. A lifetime pledge—she would be happy. I'd make sure of it. From vileness something pure.

Life had been mostly routine, but I cherished every moment in our small world. Lucy's smile was everything. I kept a baby diary, recording every milestone—her first tooth, her first steps, every little change.

Patrick came into our lives by chance. His company, Platt's Construction, was one of the companies hired to renovate the shelter we were staying in, and he was installing the new windows and doors. Ripped muscles, a handsome face, and a quiet demeanour—he kept to himself mostly, always focused on the job. Something about him drew me to him instantly.

The first time I saw him I was struck by how handsome he was. "I'm here to replace your windows. Can I come in?"

"Of course." Flustered by his gorgeous brown eyes, I smiled. "You're our first visitor."

His eyebrows raised, a curious expression crossing his chiselled features. "Well, I'm Patrick, and it's very nice to meet you both."

There was something about the warmth of his smile, the way he seemed at ease stepping into our lives.

On his second visit I'd opened the door to his broad smile. "I've brought a rattle for Lucy. I hope you don't mind." He'd placed it on the table, and then shoved his hands into his pockets seeming a little awkward.

My cheeks flushed, surely turning the same colour as my new red lipstick. "It's beautiful. You shouldn't have."

Over the days that followed, I started making lunch for him, or we'd head to the local pub for a sandwich.

"Looks like we'll be finished by the end of the week," he said one afternoon, "just snagging left to do."

"We'll miss you, won't we, Lucy?" I said, glancing at both of them. The sun warmed my new t-shirt, and my feet ached in my heels.

Lucy shook her rattle, grinning directly at Patrick.

"She likes you."

"Me too," he mumbled, blushing. "I mean, I like her mum, too."

Flushed with bravery, I stood up. "Come on, let's go and see if someone will babysit for me tonight. If you're free, of course."

Patrick jumped to his feet, a huge grin on his face. "I'm free. I'll pick you up at seven; take you to 'The Shoe'—my favourite spot."

That afternoon, I scoured the charity shops for the perfect dress and found it at Marie Curie in Knowle—a slinky, knee-length red number with a neckline at the right depth to accentuate my curves without being too revealing. Soft pleats flowing from my waist accentuated my femininity.

When Patrick arrived, his face lit up. He was dressed in smart jeans, a jacket, and polished shoes—every inch the gentleman. My heart skipped a beat.

"Nancy, you look amazing." His eyes ran over me, rubbing his hands together like he couldn't believe his luck.

It made me laugh. "I couldn't disappoint you, not for a restaurant you rave about, could I?"

That evening turned out to be perfect in every way. By the end of the evening, we were holding hands, and I knew the next move was mine.

"Come back to mine for a nightcap? I've got wine, beer—whatever you like," I offered.

"Won't we wake Lucy?"

"No." With sparkling eyes and a shy smile, I reached out and touched his arm. "She's staying at my friend Hazel's with her daughter Becky tonight, so it's just us."

Patrick smiled, more with his eyes than his lips, sending a shiver down my spine as his fingers brushed my neck while he pulled out my chair.

A whirlwind of excitement and nerves danced inside me. How had something so lucky come along? This man has a great personality and had spun my world into a new universe.

Three months after our first date, Lucy and I moved into his small cottage in Lapworth. Wasting no time, Patrick and I tied the knot as soon as our notice of intention to marry passed the twenty-nine days at the registry office. Two office clerks from the Registry Office signed as witnesses. I kept the news from my parents, fearing they'd find a way to shatter my happiness. Shortly after our rushed and hushed marriage, he adopted Lucy.

We were a family, though Patrick longed for more children—wishing Lucy had a brother or sister. But the deep-seated fear my father had planted in me ran deep, convincing me I was wicked. That Lucy was born whole, with all her fingers and toes, felt like a blessing from God. I dared not tempt His wrath by having another child, no matter how much my wonderful husband desired it. His pain pierced me deeply, but I was too emotionally scarred to take that risk.

On Lucy's first birthday, I ventured to my old home to speak to my mother. Time was healing my wounds. The door slamming on my face caused me to have a break down, spinning my delicate mental health into turmoil. Patrick was beside himself as he nursed me back to something close to normal. Rejection cuts to the quick and the best way for me to deal with it was to pretend I didn't care.

I never returned to my parents' house, not even after my father was pronounced legally dead seven years after he went missing, and my mother held a bodiless funeral. Although I never saw him again after I left home, the shame I associated with having a child never left me.

When I heard that Hazel had died from an overdose a few weeks after I moved in with Patrick, I sank into depression and loneliness. Knowing that Hazel and I had been friends, the shelter tried to contact me. I don't know what went wrong but I didn't find out until after the funeral had happened.

Becky had been placed in care, and an adoptive family found her soon after. I was inconsolable at first, but when I received a photo of Becky with her new family, I tried to find some peace. Sometimes, I'd show Lucy the picture, and she'd say, "Becky has Daddy's eyes." That always puzzled me.

Guilt filled me for years, because I hadn't adopted Becky. But I was struggling to hold it together myself. The energy it took to maintain the illusion of the perfect mother and housewife often drained me completely. Too many days I teetered on the brink, like I was hanging by a thread. My nightmares bled into my waking hours, leaving me fighting off dark thoughts that whispered I wasn't worthy, not of Lucy or Patrick, not of anyone. I struggled to keep my grip on reality, and I was afraid one day I'd lose it altogether.

My husband became my rock. Good days began to outnumber bad ones. Patrick liked to call us 'The Three Musketeers,' and I considered myself lucky, wrapped up in our little world.

Patrick purchased the construction company the year we met and I always considered that good fortune, without the company we might never have met. It had been Simon Sachwell Construction before Simon decided to retire at short notice and passed the company on to Patrick, who had 'become like a son' to him. Nobody knew why he retired at only fifty-two and when I'd asked Patrick about it he had shrugged and said he didn't know. Still, it was very lucky for us.

But when Lucy became a teenager, everything changed.

Patrick often came home, frustrated. "Why is she always crying or slamming doors? She never talks anymore."

"I don't know," I'd reply, feeling helpless. "I've tried, but you know how tight-lipped Lucy can be. She doesn't even laugh now."

"We need to talk to her teacher, find out what's going on."

"You're right, but she's thirteen—she'll hate us for interfering."

Patrick shrugged. "We need to know. Parents' evening's months away, and that could be too late."

Later that week, we turned up at St. James School and went straight to the head teacher's office.

"Welcome, Mr and Mrs Platt," Mrs Chapman greeted us warmly.

"Please call me Patrick," he said, offering a firm handshake.

We sat down, and Mrs Chapman got right to it. "You're here about Lucy, I take it?"

Patrick nodded. "She's not herself. She's sad, distant. We don't know what's going on."

"She'd be fuming if she knew we were here today," I said.

"I promise anything we say in this room, remains here." Mrs Chapman flipped through her notes, her brow furrowing. "Her grades have slipped, and her form teacher said she's withdrawn. Sometimes, she plays up. She's become rather rude to the teachers and quite the troublemaker."

Patrick sat back in his chair, frowning, though a flicker of confusion passed through his eyes. "Lucy, a troublemaker? That doesn't sit right... she's always been very polite and respectful. She's a bright girl, always had a thirst for learning."

I nodded, a dull ache settling in my chest. A piece of the puzzle clicked into place. "What about Alice? We've not seen her in ages and they used to be inseparable... are they still best friends?"

Mrs Chapman gave a small, regretful shake of her head. "I'm afraid not. Alice has grown close to Becky, a new girl who has recently joined the school. Becky doesn't like Lucy much, and it's driven a wedge between them. The friendship has come as a bit of a surprise to the teachers as Becky is two years older than Alice, but we don't interfere unless there is fighting involved."

A wave of despair rose up to drown me. They've been friends forever. I opened my mouth to speak, but Patrick gave my hand a quick squeeze, his voice calm as always. "We need to stay focused, Nancy. Let's hear all the facts."

Mrs Chapman continued, sliding a pile of papers across the desk. "Lucy's also been skipping school. She's brought in sick notes... supposedly from you."

I glanced down at the papers, my heart sinking as I recognised the forgery instantly. The handwriting wasn't mine. Tears prickled at my eyes, and I struggled to keep my voice steady. "That's not... I didn't write these."

Patrick handed me his handkerchief, his face set in quiet determination. "What can we do, Mrs Chapman?"

"I'll see if I can find Lucy a 'Buddy'. It's a new scheme we've introduced recently that seems to work very well. We ask older children to buddy up with a younger child that has problems of any sort. We'll keep an eye on her. But please, try not to overreact. She needs you to be calm and supportive."

I bit back the rising panic, nodding. "We're trying. We really are."

But inside, everything felt like it was unravelling. My little girl was slipping away, and I was powerless to stop it. *What happened to the bright, happy girl who used to share everything with me?*

Mrs Chapman's voice cut through my thoughts. "Has anything changed at home?"

Patrick shifted in his seat, his voice dropping to a quiet murmur. "I've been away more, work's been... difficult. With all the supply chain issues in construction, I've had to take on extra shifts."

"I understand." Mrs Chapman nodded sympathetically.

Patrick rubbed his temples, a deep sigh escaping him. "I'll try to be at home more. I can send one of the team on the overnight jobs for a while."

I forced a smile, though the weight on my chest hadn't lifted. "I'll see if Alice's mum will arrange a sleepover. Just the two of them. That might help."

Mrs Chapman smiled kindly as she rose from her seat. "We'll get through this together. Let's meet again in five weeks and see how things are progressing. I'll send you weekly updates."

We thanked her and left the office just as the school bell rang. Walking towards the car, I turned to Patrick, my mind racing. "Was this meeting necessary? Could it all be a misunderstanding?"

Patrick stared straight ahead, his hands tightening on the steering wheel. "There's more to it than we realise. Why doesn't this Becky like Lucy? Everyone loves her... don't they?"

*****

Over the next few years, Lucy's world crumbled bit by bit. No matter how hard Patrick and I tried to help, it was never enough.

The sleepover with Alice never happened. When I reached out, Alice's mum brushed me off with a casual, "Kids will be kids," and shut the door on any more questions. *But they've been friends forever...*

Lucy withdrew further, shrinking into herself. Her room became her fortress, the door always closed. "I'm in my room. No, I don't want dinner," she'd shout, her voice distant, cold.

"Can I run you a bath, love?" I'd offer, clinging to the hope of some connection.

"No."

Then the signs began to appear. *Do Not Disturb, Keep Out*, scrawled across her door in thick black ink. One day, she screwed a bolt to the inside of her bedroom door—something to keep me out. *Why would she need to lock me out?* Patrick was secretly impressed with her handywoman skills; I could have thumped him.

I'd listen to her stomp around upstairs, belting out songs at the top of her voice, and I'd crumple into the sofa, beating the cushions in frustration. "Patrick, she hates me. I can't do anything right. I'm the enemy."

He'd pull me close, his tired eyes soft with reassurance. "She'll come around. It's just a phase."

But the deep lines around his eyes, the weariness in his voice, told me he wasn't so sure. I bit my lip, forcing a smile. "I hope you're right."

Patrick chuckled, patting his bulging waistline. "Now where's my lunch, woman? I've got to be back at work in twenty minutes."

"Oh, you and your stomach!" Though my banter remained light, my heart wasn't in it.

We muddled through, but things never improved. Lucy ate everything in sight, yet never gained weight. She'd disappear to the bathroom right after every meal, and her mood swings... they were sharp, unpredictable.

"I think Lucy might be bulimic," I whispered one night. "She's hiding something. She's always wearing that cardigan, even when it's warm." My voice caught as I remembered the thin red lines I'd glimpsed on her arms when she'd taken off her cardigan while washing up. "I saw cuts... I tried to ask her, but she ran upstairs."

Patrick's brow furrowed. "Self-harming? Nancy, are you sure?"

I nodded, swallowing the lump in my throat. "She's hurting. I don't know what to do."

He exhaled slowly, his hand rubbing the back of his neck. "I'll take her to work with me. Keep her busy. Maybe that'll help."

Relief washed over me, if only for a moment. "What would I do without you?"

From then on, every weekend, Lucy worked with Patrick at Platt's, helping with bookkeeping and admin. She was good at it, brilliant even. "She's got the gift of the gab," Patrick said one day, his voice filled with rare pride. "The customers love her."

Lucy, leaning against the doorframe, rolled her eyes. "Dad, they'd love anyone who could keep up with the paperwork."

Patrick smirked. "True. Lucy's nothing special."

Her face fell, and she stared at her feet. The hurt was instant, like a slap.

"Oh, you want praise, do you?" Patrick ribbed. "Daddy's little girl isn't being very nice to Mummy, is she?"

Lucy shuffled uncomfortably, glancing at me with guilt in her eyes before looking away again. Rejection made my cheeks flush crimson, bringing on a mix of frustration and heartache. *Why can't I reach her?*

I forced a smile, my voice soft. "Love... we just want what's best for you."

"I know, Mum," she mumbled. "Sorry for how I've been."

I wrapped her in a hug, though the embrace felt fragile, temporary. Patrick gave me a reassuring smile over her shoulder, but I wasn't convinced. Holding onto my daughter compared to greased hands catching an eel—impossible.

Briefly, life settled. Lucy made an effort, came down for meals and spent more time with us. It was during that fragile peace that I had an idea—a surprise, something to bring her back to us fully.

One morning, I bellowed up to her room. "Lucy, there's a special delivery for you!"

A thud from above told me she'd fallen out of bed. "What is it?" she grumbled, wiping sleep from her eyes as she padded downstairs. "I'm not at school today. I was having a lie-in."

"Well, we think you'll love it," Patrick chimed in, standing by the kitchen table, trying to suppress a grin. "But hey, what do we know? We're only your parents."

In the middle of the table sat a small cardboard box, tied up with a bright red ribbon and a velvet bow.

Lucy's eyes widened. "Is that for me?"

"Yes, all yours. But don't shake it."

Patrick chuckled as I shot him a playful glare. "Let her open it, Patrick."

Lucy's fingers trembled as she pulled the box towards her, cutting the ribbon and untying the bow. Her face froze as a soft rustling sound came from inside. "What was that?"

The box moved, just a little. Her mouth dropped open as two bewildered brown eyes peeked up at her. She gasped, her hands flying to her mouth. "Is it...?"

With shaking hands, she lifted the tiny bundle of fur from the box. The little pup wriggled in her arms, licking her face with tiny, eager kisses. Lucy's face lit up with a joy I hadn't seen in years. "Oh my God, I can't believe it!" Excited, loving arms cradled the puppy.

Patrick and I watched, grinning like idiots. We laughed until our sides ached, the tension of the past years momentarily forgotten.

"He's a Border Collie," I explained. "Ten weeks old. The shyest of the litter."

Lucy smiled down at the puppy, stroking his fur. "He's like me... we'll be best friends."

Patrick lifted the camera, snapping a photo. The pride in his eyes was unmistakable, though only I knew how much it weighed on him. Capturing the moment, I let a tear slip down my cheek. *Maybe we're finally getting her back.*

"I see you're happy Nancy! Do you want a whole box of tissues?" said Patrick tongue in cheek.

Lucy looked up at me, eyes shining. "Thank you, Mum. Thank you, Dad."

"What will you call him, Baby Girl?" Patrick asked, still holding the camera.

"Rufus," she said, her voice full of certainty. "Definitely Rufus."

The puppy tilted his head, as if considering the name, then let out a small yelp, sealing the decision.

From that moment, Lucy and Rufus were inseparable. He'd wait for her at the window every day after school, and at night, he'd curl up at the foot of her bed. In fits and starts, we began to see glimmers of the old Lucy. She came back to us, piece by piece, and for the first time in years, I allowed myself to hope.

*****

Had I known how brief our break from our combative daughter would be, I'd have cherished every moment. Instead, I slipped back into my routine as a house-proud worker and full-time gardener. I should have swapped lunch with friends for mother-and-daughter time at home. And rather than shouting when Lucy sent Rufus crashing through my flower beds, I'd have put down my tools and chased that wild dog with her.

Alas, we don't have hindsight until it's too late.

At sixteen, Lucy transformed into someone I didn't recognised. Black clothes—oversized and shapeless—swallowed her thin frame. Her once vibrant hair had been dyed a dreadful inky black that made her skin a ghostly white. Thick black eyeliner circled her eyes, and her lips were always coated in dark, dramatic lipstick. She wore a ring through her nose, a glaring symbol of rebellion that made me nauseous every time I saw it.

"Why on earth have you dyed your hair? It drains your colour." I know I sounded exasperated but I couldn't help myself.

"I love it," she shot back. "People actually notice me now."

Frustration mixed with helplessness. "You already have such lovely hair, clothes, makeup... why all this?"

"You're *so* out of touch, Mum. Get a life."

Rufus ignored the change and loved her unconditionally, but Lucy's resentment towards us became undeniable. She couldn't stand the life we'd provided, though she'd benefitted from it well enough. I couldn't understand it. She was smart and talented—her soprano voice earned her a spot in the school choir. Of course, she hated that too, storming out in a fit a few weeks after starting.

If she'd lived in my shoes, gone through what I went through, then she'd have cause to throw tantrums. Everything, we'd given her, and this was our thanks. Childhood for me had been awful. Not allowed make-up or pretty clothes, with an indifferent mother and an indecent father, I knew how dreadful life can be. If anyone needed to 'act up' it should be me! Lucy had no idea what hardship was.

Get a life? I had a life, a beautiful one which was currently being pulled apart by my spoilt daughter—the love of my life and my reason for living.

Now, she'd joined a local band, *Black Maria,* who practised in a disused railway station in Lapworth. I'd heard rumours about marijuana and how they were an odd lot, but at least she seemed happier.

When we found out she was dating Jeff, the guitarist come singer, a cold dread settled in my chest. Six years older, strung out, unwashed—he was bad news. Patrick and I were both on edge about it, but what could we do? Lucy was headstrong, and anything we said would push her further away.

Then came the event we had been dreading.

"Patrick, come home," I said, trying to keep my voice steady. "Lucy's gone. She's living rough with Jeff at the railway station."

He stayed calm, though I could hear the strain in his voice. "She'll get tired of it, love. She'll miss home, and Rufus, especially."

"Do you think so?" My heart skipped a beat with hope.

"Of course. She can't stay out there forever."

Rufus sat at the window every day, waiting for her. He'd glance at us when we called his name, but his gaze always returned to the street, expecting her to walk through the door. He was as stubborn as she was.

As the weeks stretched into months, the cold weather crept in, and my mind buzzed with worry. University, her mental health, everything—it was all too much. I couldn't stand it. We asked her to come home. But she insisted that 'waste of space' come with her. I wanted to scream, but Patrick, ever the strategist, convinced me to let it happen.

For a while, things seemed... manageable. Jeff helped in the garden and Lucy returned to studying. Rufus bounced back to life, wagging his tail, bringing his ball to everyone in the hope of a game, though he was banished downstairs because the new 'freeloading lodger' didn't like dogs.

But it didn't last. Lucy's weight kept dropping, the familiar signs of her bulimia resurfacing.

"Lucy, you're getting thin again. Do you need to see the doctor?"

"Not now, Mum. Everything's under control." Her tone was clipped, final.

I knew better than to push, but it worried me sick, seeing her slip back into old patterns.

And then there was Jeff. His trips to the railway station grew more frequent, and Lucy's anxiety grew in parallel. She'd fidget, her eyes darting nervously whenever he was late. When she gave up studying altogether and began following him everywhere, a chasm opened between us.

Jeff, always dishevelled and bleary-eyed, would come home with flimsy excuses—pollen allergies, he'd say. I pretended to believe him. It was easier than confronting the truth, but he was dragging Lucy down with him.

One night, they came home, and my heart stopped. Lucy was barely standing. Bruised, her hair matted with dried blood, clumps missing, her face swollen. She limped across the threshold, each step drawn in pain. My blood boiled.

"What on earth happened, Lucy?" I rushed over, my voice shaking.

Jeff interjected, too quickly. "She's clumsy, aren't you, Babe?"

Lucy nodded, but she wouldn't meet my eyes. She stared at the floor, hiding behind the lie.

He went on, spinning some ridiculous story about an embankment and strangers helping her. But I saw right through it. His clothes were spotless; hers were filthy. It didn't make sense.

When Patrick got home, I told him everything, and we both knew it was nonsense.

That night at dinner, I forced a smile, dishing out the meals. Jeff got a vegan dish, while the rest of us had chicken. Patrick kept the conversation light, pretending not to notice Lucy flinch with every movement.

"So, Jeff, what's new at the railway station?"

"The usual. Becky's been sprucing it up with flowers and incense, making it cosy for us. It's proper vibey now." Jeff forced a cheerful grin.

Lucy hunched over her plate, avoiding eye contact. I watched her wince, each movement clearly causing her pain. I wanted to grab her and shake her free from whatever hold he had over her.

Patrick, always one to play the long game, finished his meal and turned to Jeff. "How about helping me with some heavy lifting at the depot? I'll drop you back at the station after."

Jeff's grin faltered but he nodded. "Sure, Patrick. You don't mind, do you, Babe?"

She didn't raise her head. "No, it's fine."

Later that evening, when Patrick returned, he handed me a glass of wine. I could tell from his face something had shifted.

Lucy walked in on us, worry making her frown. "Where's Jeff?"

"I dropped him off at the station. He seemed fine." Patrick's casual tone didn't match the look he gave me.

Lucy's brow furrowed in confusion. "He's forgotten his guitar. He never forgets his guitar."

Patrick shrugged. "I don't know, love. But that's what he said. I'm sure he'll manage."

I could tell from Lucy's face that she was confused. "Come on. Let's have an early night."

"Okay. I'm not feeling too good, to be honest."

In the quiet of the night, the soft echo of her footsteps carried through the house. I listened as she paced, haunted by her demons. I ached to go to her, to offer words of comfort and reassurance, but I knew she didn't want them. The sting of her rejection pierced deeper than I'd care to admit, as it always did. I turned away, pulling Patrick closer. Family meant everything to both of us, but sometimes, it felt like it was slipping through our fingers.

Chapter 8

Nancy—Behind Closed Doors

HELPING LUCY rebuild her life wasn't easy for any of us. Every time the phone rang, she'd rush to answer, only to storm around the house afterwards, slamming doors and tearing through the cupboards for something to eat. Her frustration was palpable, but she rarely spoke about it.

Patrick remained hopeful. "She'll get over him. He's never coming back."

"If only we could be sure."

"You have my concrete word on it," he'd say, adding a wink as if that alone would make it true.

After a while, Lucy began to accept that Jeff had gone. She never said it outright, but word spread that he'd left Lapworth with Becky, the same girl who supposedly 'helped' Lucy after her fall. I never believed that story.

With painfully slow progress, Lucy found her way back to herself. Reflecting her inner stability she'd returned to her natural hair colouring, and with no caked on foundation, her freckles danced across her cheeks and nose for all to see. She threw herself into her studies, earning straight A's and securing a place at Oxford. Three years later, Patrick and I attended her Degree Ceremony, standing proudly as she smiled among her friends, her arm linked with her new boyfriend, Jordan. That smile of hers could launch a thousand ships; she radiated happiness.

Patrick leaned in and said, "Jordan's impressive. Much better than Jeff, and his dad's a professor at Cambridge University."

"I know." Though, in all honesty, something about Jordan made me uneasy. "There's an edge to him. I can't explain it, but he only seems pleasant when things are going his way. I wouldn't want to cross him." A chill ran through me.

Patrick pulled at his collar, where his neck had red blotches. "Don't be a spoilsport. Lucy's happy, and that's what matters."

Grudgingly, I agreed. "You're right, as usual. Must be a mother's intuition."

He smiled, "You and your intuition."

"It's never failed me yet."

He wiped his brow with his handkerchief. "Let's savour this moment, shall we?"

"Take off your jacket, Patrick. You're roasting."

"No love, I'll grin and bear it. Got short sleeves on—you know how I feel about my tattoos."

"They're fine to me," I said, my gaze trailing over him.

Patrick chuckled. "Not now, Nancy. We're with the fancy crowd today."

*****

Life moved quickly after that. When Lucy and Jordan decided to move in together near us, I was thrilled. But with the property market sky-high, they would struggle to find a place within their budget.

"Let's give them the money," I suggested to Patrick. "Better now while we can see them enjoy it."

"The business isn't doing well just now… but yes, let's help them. My Baby Girl deserves the best house money can buy."

Lucy and Jordan were ecstatic. The rambling Victorian house in Earlswood was perfect. They were grateful when we paid for it outright and promised to help cover the renovation costs as well.

Jordan tried to be cautious. "Platt's Construction must be doing well, Patrick. Don't overstretch yourself. Let us take on the mortgage. Lucy and I both have good jobs."

Patrick waved it off. "You might as well have the money now rather than wait. We want to see you happy."

Jordan smiled. "Thanks, Patrick. Don't worry, I'll look after Lucy."

Patrick grinned. "Good. Wedding and babies next, for my little girl."

Jordan shifted, uncomfortable. "Bit cart before the horse, eh?"

Patrick told me about that conversation later, and we were both left uneasy. Luckily, we'd put the house in our names, letting them live there rent free until they got married—then it would become our wedding present. I hadn't agreed with Patrick at first over that aspect, but now I'm relieved.

Despite the nagging voice in my head telling me that not everything was well, Lucy and Jordan portrayed an idyllic life.

We visited most weekends, strolling around the nearby lakes together, enjoying the calm. It was a magical time, and we pushed any concerns to the back of our minds.

Lucy thrived at Hargrove & Collins Financial Services in Birmingham, while Jordan struggled at Adams Accountants. Yet they hosted dinner parties for his colleagues, always aiming to impress. Lucy and I would spend hours crafting elaborate meals—escargots, strawberry bisque, salmon medallions, duck à l'orange, beef Wellington. The desserts were a feast of fruits, pies, and cheeses.

"How did the evening go?" I'd ask. "The food looked amazing."

"The food was fine, but the evening? A disaster. Jordan's colleagues don't like me. I was excluded, ignored."

I tried to reassure her. "Surely not. You're wonderful with people, and you looked fantastic."

Lucy's eyes brimmed with tears. "According to Jordan, I dress like you, Mum. No offence."

Her words stung, but I forced a smile. "No worries. We'll go shopping this weekend." Reaching up, I touched her long brown hair, an inward sigh escaping me. Soft and natural, it framed her face so much better than the dyed black Goth phase she'd gone through. I hoped she'd keep it this way, keep herself this way. Her hair always mirrored her emotions—shifting shades in step with her inner turmoil.

Patrick and I grew more concerned over time. Jordan was often out when we arrived, the back door slamming just as we walked in. Lucy covered for him—"He's meeting the lads for squash," or "he's working late." The excuses never ended.

Lucy began to struggle. After nine months, she quit her job, and we stepped in, offering gifts and a generous allowance to help her stay afloat. But something was off, and whenever we tried to talk to her, she shut us down. It was clear Jordan wasn't offering the support she needed, but Lucy wouldn't admit it.

Cardigans had turned into her uniform—oversized, shapeless, swallowing her frame. A far cry from the vibrant woman she once radiated. I could still hear her at twenty, laughing as she said, "Nothing makes you look older than a too-large cardigan, Mum. Promise me you'll never buy me one."

I hadn't. But now, seeing her wrapped in those baggy clothes, I knew something had gone terribly wrong.

That night, I wanted to bring it up with Patrick, but when we pulled into the drive, he didn't move.

"Aren't you coming in?"

"No. All this time at Lucy's... it's left me behind at work. I don't want you to worry, but I've lost a few jobs recently."

"Oh, no. Why didn't you tell me? Do you want me to come into the office and help?"

His face softened, the lines around his eyes easing. "No, love. The office isn't the issue. I've dropped the ball, and I need to sort it. Go on inside, and don't wait up."

We leaned in for the usual kiss, the kind that meant nothing. My eyes burned, but I blinked it away. "See you later, then."

By 3:30 a.m., I still stood at the window, staring blankly at the empty drive. He'd come home when he was ready, smelling of perfume, after another one-night stand. The hurt? That had long since faded into something numb, something I'd never let him know about. These nights out were his release valve, his way of unloading whatever he carried.

But what cut deepest wasn't his drinking or the women. It was the way our friends drifted away, too ashamed to be seen with us anymore. That ate away at me more than anything else.

*****

For over two months, Lucy had been fobbing me off with one excuse or another as to why we couldn't have a get-together. Fed up with the excuses, and worried sick, I decided to turn up unannounced.

Not knowing what kind of reception I would receive, my hand shook as I rang the doorbell. When Lucy opened the door, I tried to sound as cheerful as possible. "Hello, Darling! Surprise, surprise—we're off for a spa day, compliments of Dad."

Her tear-streaked face and dark, sunken eyes stopped me cold. "Mum, I can't go out today."

One look at her crumpled, blood-stained pyjamas and greasy hair and I pushed past her and walked in. "What's wrong, love?"

"Nothing," Lucy whimpered, her eyes flicking nervously toward the clock.

"Come here." I held my arms open, patting the sofa beside me.

She collapsed into my embrace, and immediately, a sharp, familiar pain formed at the base of my skull—a migraine creeping in, deep and throbbing. The kind I had when something was terribly wrong.

"I can't do anything right, Mum," she sobbed against my shoulder. "The house is disgusting, and so am I. It's written all over your face. You're repulsed."

"Of course not," I soothed, though my heart ached seeing her this way. "Where's all this coming from?"

Leaning in closer, her voice muffled, "Jordan calls me useless. Tells me I can't even keep the house clean and that I smell like a skunk."

I glanced around the room. It didn't seem that bad, nothing that couldn't be tidied up. But she pulled me up by the hand, leading me to the bedroom.

Clothes littered the floor in heaps, the duvet was a crumpled mess, and dirty laundry was strewn everywhere. Dust had settled thickly on the dressing table; you could practically write your name in it.

"See what I mean?" Her defiance melting into sobs as she sank to the floor, curling up beneath the window.

I knelt beside her, my heart breaking with every tear that fell. "Darling, it's not as bad as you think. Go and take a shower, change into something fresh. We'll go to Moreton's for lunch, maybe pick up Rufus on the way."

She shook her head violently, panic rising in her voice. "I can't leave it like this. Jordan said it had to be sorted today." Her body trembled, breath coming in shallow, rapid gasps.

"Calm down, love. I'll get Janet and her team to come over and tidy up for you."

A fragile hope returned to her eyes. "Would you do that for me?"

I nodded, watching as the tension began to ease from her face. Slowly, the colour returned to her cheeks, though the mascara marks beneath her eyes remained as stark reminders of her pain. There was something behind her smile, a lost, distant look that I couldn't quite place. I'd ask her about it later, over drinks.

An hour later, we sat at Moreton's, the warm clatter of plates and chatter around us offering a brief respite. I needed answers.

Needing her to open up, I kept my voice gentle, "So, why are you so sad?"

"It's my hormones. The doctor's given me estrogen patches to combat the mood swings, but they're not really working." She couldn't meet my eyes and her voice lacked conviction.

"That's not the truth, is it?"

She hesitated, her fingers nervously tracing the rim of her glass. "I can't say any more."

I decided it wasn't the time to push. It was too raw, too close to whatever was eating her from the inside. I'd find out soon enough.

Back at home that evening, I told Patrick what little I knew. But more importantly, at what I guessed was going on, knowing it was the stuff Lucy hid from me that worried me most. He paced the room, fists clenched, knocking over a chair in his anger. Even Rufus couldn't settle him.

"That bastard's going to pay for what he's been doing to our Baby Girl."

*****

A few weeks later, the phone rang, blood draining out of my face the moment I heard Lucy's voice.

Muffled and sobbing, making it hard to understand her. "Mum... I'm locked in the wardrobe."

My blood ran cold. I hung up immediately and rushed to her house, fury pounding in my veins. When I got there, I didn't knock; I let myself in with the spare key and then ran up the stairs two at a time. After a quick assessment, I propped up my mobile and put it to record while I set about beating the death out of the door lock. Each bang a desperate attempt to get to her, with me imagining the lock was Jordan's smug, cruel face.

When Lucy opened up, the truth came pouring out in gasps and sobs. I listened, seething. Jordan's words, his actions—everything I'd feared had come true. I telephoned Patrick right away, demanding he come and change the locks on the house right away.

"I've never been prouder of my girls," he said, his voice heavy with emotion.

Later, after Lucy confronted Jordan, we all agreed on a plan. We never reported him to the police as we had threatened, there was no need. He wouldn't hurt her again.

*****

When Lucy moved to London, it gave Patrick and I the space to focus on ourselves. We rebuilt our lives, our business, and our love. Somehow, out of the ashes, we found a new beginning. Rufus was always by our side, and slowly, Platt's began to thrive again. The late nights, the smell of cheap perfume clinging to Patrick's suits—those days were behind us.

Patrick's wandering eye had been a shadow in our marriage, one I had grown used to, even if it had stung more often than I'd admit. But deep down, I always believed he would come back to me, that one day I'd be enough. I never confronted him, never tried to pin him down. I knew how men like him were. They needed their distractions, fleeting as they were.

I was patient, and over time, it paid off. The thrill of those other women faded, and now, in the quiet of our home, it was me he turned to, me who filled his thoughts. I had always known he would settle, and now, my patience bore fruit and my cup overflowed.

We still lived for any news of Lucy. She was our pride, our joy, and though she was far away, she was finding herself again. We grew hopeful that the change would do her good.

"She's working in a cocktail bar in Canary Wharf," I told Patrick one evening. "She's got a loft apartment which she loves."

"That's our girl," Patrick said, smiling. "I knew she'd make us proud."

"We'll have to go down to see her," I said wistfully, staring at the photo of Lucy on my phone, her short blonde bob and new bohemian look radiating through the screen. I missed her chestnut hair but she looked so happy it didn't matter.

"Give her time, Nancy. She'll invite us down soon, I'm sure."

I passed him my phone. "Look at her. She's amazing."

Patrick rubbed his eyes, his voice softening. "She really is. She's filled out a bit, hasn't she? Looks healthier."

"Yes, she's back to a size ten." I smiled, though a pang of worry twisted inside me. "Do you think she's healing on the inside?"

“Yes, my love, I do.” Patrick’s tone was reassuring, his hand squeezing mine before changing the subject. “Have you seen her reviews on Trip Advisor? Five stars for Molecular Mixology.”

His pride was palpable, and I couldn’t help but giggle as he puffed out his chest like a proud father. “Put me down, won’t you?” I laughed as he swept me off my feet. “Lucy’s got my taste for a good drink, Patrick. She takes after me.”

“Alright, alright. A Spiced Rum and Coke it is then.” He grinned, heading to the drinks cabinet. “Bit early, though, isn’t it?”

“Celebrating Lucy’s success is never too early!”

“I’ll join you with a beer, then.” Patrick raised his bottle. “And maybe an early night?”

“You’re so predictable.” But I laughed as we clinked our glasses.

*****

We hadn’t heard much from Lucy for a while, but everything seemed to be going well. She sounded happier than we could have hoped for. Then, one morning, a card arrived in the post—she was moving in with a man called Daniel. I telephoned her as soon as I read the card.

I tried to keep my voice light, though my curiosity got the better of me. “So, who’s Daniel? And why are we only just hearing about him now?”

“Sorry, Mum. It’s been manic.” Lucy sounded flustered. “Daniel’s amazing. You’ll love him, I promise.”

“Well, what does he do?”

“He’s a PE teacher at a school nearby.”

“That’s a great job, but I have to ask…”

“Go on then,” Lucy said, sighing in that way only daughters can.

“How can you both afford a penthouse in Canary Wharf? PE teachers don’t make that kind of money, Lucy, and unless you’ve changed jobs, neither do you.”

“Mum, it’s fine. Daniel has savings, and I got a raise.”

I could tell she was getting defensive, so I bit my lip, but not before letting out an involuntary ‘tut.’

“Mum,” Lucy’s voice softened, “you and Dad should come over this weekend. Meet Daniel. You’ll see, everything’s fine.”

“We can’t wait, Darling,” I said, forcing a smile into my words, though my mind was already racing.

*****

When the weekend arrived, Patrick and I set off to meet this Daniel and see their new home. The drive stretched on endlessly, an uneasy silence hanging between us. Patrick hummed along to the radio, tapping the steering wheel, but my thoughts wandered. Who was this Daniel? What kind of man had swept Lucy into a penthouse of all places?

My nerves tightened with every passing mile, my fingers drumming on my knee and not to the beat of the music. An eerie awareness curled through me, winding me as tight as a coiled spring ready to snap.

By the time we reached Canary Wharf, I had palpitations. Staying composed, to keep Patrick from noticing, took a lot of effort. The tower loomed above us—sleek, impersonal—nothing like the warm, inviting home I’d envisioned for Lucy.

We stepped inside, and I couldn’t help but admire the space, though a chill lingered beneath the polished surfaces. “What a fabulous place, Baby Girl,” Patrick said, glancing around. “What does Daniel do again?”

I hardly heard him. My eyes darted around, searching for something—anything—that felt like my daughter.

"He's a PE teacher, Dad. Surely Mum told you?"

"Oh, yes," Patrick said distractedly. "I've been up to my neck in work and walking Rufus these days."

"I miss Rufus so much," Lucy said, her voice softening. "We'll come up to see you both soon."

"That would be lovely," Patrick replied, though I could see his eyes roaming the room, taking in the lavish furnishings, the new curtains, and—oddly—a roll of cash sitting casually on the side table.

"Ted's had a makeover, hasn't he?" Patrick said, pointing at Lucy's old stuffed toy, now looking pristine, perched neatly on a chair.

"Yes," Lucy beamed. "Daniel had him fixed up as a surprise for me. He's so thoughtful."

A smile tugged at my lips, her enthusiasm contagious. "Are you still working at The Al-Chemist?" My voice stayed calm, though tension prickled beneath my skin, the unshakable sense that something bad hovered just beyond reach.

"Yes, Mum." Lucy's expression dropped. "We're fine, honestly. What is it with you two? You're always looking for the worst."

"We're not," Patrick interjected, sharing a quick look with me. "We're just worried about you, that's all."

Lucy smiled at us, the tension easing. "Anyway, here he is—the love of my life," she announced, rushing to open the door as Daniel came in.

Patrick and I exchanged a quick glance as we watched Lucy place slippers on the mat for him, a gesture strangely submissive for our daughter.

Daniel waved her off with a smile. "No need for that today, Lu." A West Country twang mixed with West Indies and London and gave him a distinctly unique accent.

We both gave Daniel the once-over. His tracksuit was expensive, his trainers spotless, and the gold necklace around his neck gleamed. I couldn't help but feel a pang of discomfort.

"Hello, Patrick, Nancy," Daniel said, flashing us a grin. "Or should I call you Mum and Dad?"

Patrick shook his hand firmly. "Let's stick with Patrick and Nancy."

"Nice place you have here," I said, trying to make conversation, though I couldn't stop myself from eyeing his gold chain again.

"Fit for a princess," Daniel wrapped his arm around Lucy. "That's what I always tell her."

Lucy snorted, and the two of them burst out laughing. Patrick and I joined in, though our laughter felt more like an effort to mask our unease than shared joy.

As we toured the penthouse, I took in all the small, telling details that told me Lucy didn't fit in here.

Ted, almost unrecognizable, looked like a brand-new bear. For some strange reason, Lucy had always taken comfort in Ted's distressed state. I'd assumed if he looked worse than her that made her feel like she was doing okay. Seeing Ted repaired sent a shiver down my spine.

"Ted's looking very dapper," I said, trying to keep my tone light.

"That's me," Daniel said, chuckling. "I couldn't stand the sight of him all tattered and torn."

"Poor old Ted." I glanced at Lucy. Her cheeks flushed pink, and I could tell she was trying to laugh it off, but there was something guarded about her now.

Patrick shot me a warning look, his eyes telling me to hold my tongue.

"Come on, love. Let's make some coffee."

Lucy followed me into the kitchen and I went to put the kettle on.

"We use the De'Longhi, it only makes two cups at a time but it's really good coffee. Here let me show you."

Feigning interest, I rubbed shoulders with her and gave her a big grin. Though a nagging inside me grew stronger with each moment, something wasn't right, but now wasn't the time to confront it.

Chapter 9

Patrick—Weight of Deceit and Responsibility

MEETING NANCY turned everything around. Before her, life had felt like I was running in the slow lane, but with her by my side, I grew into the man I always knew I could be. Lucy was the icing on the cake—gangly legs, dimpled smile, and eyes that lit up like no one else's.

The early years rolled by filled with golden memories, and though I'd have liked a brother or sister for Lucy, it never happened. With sensitive questions, I'd bring it up from time to time, but Nancy would always push back. "I don't deserve more children, for what I did. You could do so much better than me, I will understand if you want to leave." Her voice always carried a hint of finality.

I tried to soften it. "Don't be daft. You were only a child yourself."

Her eyes would cloud over, her gaze far away. "I should have told Mum," she'd sigh, like she hadn't heard me at all.

When her parents found out Nancy was pregnant, they threw her out, and that's when I found her. The best thing that ever happened to me, renovating the shelter back then.

Nancy had this quietness about her—soft-spoken, shy, and so thin she looked like the wind could knock her down. But there was strength too. That killer smile, that throaty laugh, they lit up the room, especially when Lucy was nearby.

You'd never guess by looking at her that she'd ended up in the shelter, not with the way she stood out from the other girls, with her rosary beads draped on the mantel. I knew Hazel was a crackhead, but Nancy… Nancy had something different, a story she kept hidden from the world in the missing pieces.

In time, she let some of it out. "Strict Catholics," she'd said once, a bitterness in her tone. "I was their disgrace. My mum never looked at me the same after that. They told me to never darken their door again."

"What about Lucy's father?"

She'd shake her head, giving me that look like I should know better than to pry. "He did a runner, I think." And then, as if the subject had never come up, she'd flash a smile, touch my knee, and ask where we were eating for lunch. I let it slide. Whatever secrets she had, I didn't need to drag them out. She was mine now, and I was happy with my girls.

But the shadows stayed. Even after all those years, Nancy woke up drenched in sweat, nightmares wrapping around her like a vice. In her sleep, she'd murmur things I didn't want to hear or understand. Words like, "Don't tell your mother," and "It's our little secret," made me want to dig up her father's grave and finish what death already had. But it was too late for that.

Lucy, well, she had her own struggles. My fears of inherited mental disorders flowed with her every smile and frown. Always a loner, that girl. Friends came and went, never sticking around long enough to make a real difference. She was on the outside, looking in, and no matter how much Nancy and I tried to reach her, it never seemed enough. The slamming doors, the tears—it felt like we were losing her bit by bit.

Then Jeff appeared, and Lucy's spark came back. I knew exactly what was going on in that derelict station they'd holed up in. Even the rats had given it a pass. But I kept my mouth shut. At least she was smiling again.

"So where's the gig tonight, love?" I'd ask, trying to keep the conversation light.

"The Shoe," she'd reply, her grin stretching wide. "You and Mum coming?"

"Wouldn't miss it."

That smile of hers could've lit up the darkest room, but I took my chance. "Have you thought about coming home? Cold's setting in and Rufus misses you too."

She sighed. "I miss him too. He's such a good boy."

"So, what do you think?" I pressed.

"I'd want Jeff to come, but Mum won't agree to that."

"You and your imagination. Leave your mother to me." Hopeful optimism made me think, *this time will be different.*

A week later, I walked in to find Jeff in the garden mowing the lawn, and Lucy and Nancy laughing in the kitchen. Lucy gave me a quick hug as she walked past with her cup of coffee and went off to continue studying. Everything had fallen into place. I hadn't seen her that relaxed in ages, and I started to believe maybe, just maybe, things were turning around.

But it didn't last. A phone call from Nancy came just days later.

"Love, are you sitting down?"

"Yes, what's up?"

Her voice was shaky, like she'd been crying. "Lucy's home… she's black and blue. He's done something to her."

Everything went cold inside me. "You're kidding me."

"She's limping. He said she fell down an embankment, but he's lying. I know it. He's spotless, not a scratch on him."

"I'm leaving now." Slamming the phone down released none of my anger.

Sarah, my secretary, looked up from her computer. "Everything okay, Mr Platt?"

"A bit of a family emergency. Stop all calls and you can go home early. Before you do, ask the guys to leave the Earlswood job. I'll pop by later and finish off for the weekend. I'll see you on Monday."

Sarah took off her glasses and looked up with interest. "Sorry to hear of an emergency. Is there anything I can do to help?"

"No, but thanks for offering."

Sarah stood up and started packing her desk away. "I'll clear up here and ring the guys, Mr Platt."

The drive home was a blur of swearing and honking, my thoughts racing as fast as the car. When I pulled up after the car ride from hell, I had to pause, breathe. Storming in wouldn't help.

Inside, Lucy sat on the sofa, her face a swollen mess, bruises running like dark ink under her eyes. The scumbag sat nearby, cool as you like, spinning his yellow-livered lie.

"She fell. Becky and I pulled her out of the ditch."

Lucy nodded; her voice small. "Yeah, Dad, it's true. You know how clumsy I am."

Clenching my fists, I looked at her. "You sure about that, Baby Girl?"

Her eyes flicked to Jeff. She wasn't fooling me. As I held her hand, rough from dirt and torn at the edges, I forced a smile at Jeff. "How about helping me out at the site later? You free?"

He puffed up his chest like I'd given him a badge of honour. "Sure thing. I can come now. Would you be able to drop me off at the station when we're finished?"

"Of course." I nodded, playing along. But my mind was already racing, forming a plan. One way or another, Jeff was about to learn what happened when you hurt my Baby Girl.

Half an hour later we were on our way. "Not taking your guitar with you tonight then?" I kept my tone light, though my mind had already wandered far beyond the conversation.

"Nah, not tonight. Just some beers, maybe a takeaway if I'm hungry later."

I nodded, keeping my eyes on the road ahead. "Right then, let's crack on with Earlswood. The sooner we're done, the better."

Jeff shifted in his seat. "What's the job?"

"Cementing," I said. "Need to finish it before it sets."

*****

Lucy was already pacing when I got home later that night. Her restlessness hung in the air, her footsteps tapping a rhythm I knew well. She couldn't sleep, waiting for him—that waster.

The next day, she drove straight down to the old railway station, but Jeff wasn't there. And neither was Becky.

The second Lucy stepped into the doorway of my study; I saw how strung out she was. Her eyes pinned me down, jaw clenched tight. Arms folded, her whole body coiled like a cat ready to spring. "Where did you drop him last night, Dad?" The tension in her voice sliced through the air. "The guys said he didn't turn up."

I met her gaze, steady and unflinching. "Outside, like we agreed."

"Did you see him go in?"

I paused. "No, he was talking to someone out front."

Her eyes narrowed. "Was it a woman?"

I shrugged. "Could've been. They had a woolly hat on. Someone small, slight."

I saw the flicker in her expression—hurt, anger, something else. I tried to soften the blow. "They were arguing, though. Voices were raised. Whoever it was they were pushing him."

A strange satisfaction spread across her face. There were no more questions. Instead, she began whistling that tune she used to hum as a child. Still, she clung to hope, her phone glued to her hand whenever it rang. Every day, she wandered back to that disused station, searching for a sign of him.

Nancy shook her head when I told her. "You've given her hope."

"What was I supposed to do?" I sighed. "I couldn't stand to see her like that. All bruised, eyes so sad."

"Don't make things up. Let her come to terms with it on her own. He's not coming back."

*****

Oxford University was the kind of place that demanded excellence with a quiet arrogance, where tradition and intellect intertwined, and the history of centuries hung in the air, reminding you that brilliance here was the norm, not the exception. That Lucy came here filled every inch of me with pride, sometimes so much so I thought I might burst.

Always suspicious of anyone who came near my daughter, I'd been watching Jordan closely. Charming enough on the surface, with that polished air that money could buy, but underneath it all, there was something too smooth, too practiced. Still, for Lucy, he ticked all the right boxes.

"I like Jordan." Putting my hands behind my head, I leaned back in the chair. "He's perfect for Lucy."

Nancy smiled, her face softening. "They're a good match, aren't they? Studied together, got jobs lined up. What more could we ask for?"

I rubbed my hands together, already thinking ahead. "We're moving up in the world, love. A union with his family? Could be good for business, you know?"

Nancy shook her head, laughing softly. "As if you care about anything more than you care for Lucy."

"Well, they'll need support, won't they? If a baby comes along…"

She nudged me. "You're getting ahead of yourself. Again."

"I saw you looking at those wedding magazines the other day," I teased.

She blushed, caught out. "Oh, fiddle! I thought I hid those."

"I came home early, remember?"

Her eyes twinkled. "Oh yes, now I do."

We laughed, but beneath the banter, there was something real. We both wanted the best for Lucy, always had.

I offered Nancy my arm. "Let's go and meet the prospective in-laws." She giggled as she hooked her arm through mine.

Introductions with Jordan's family went smoothly, though after only two minutes they made their excuses to leave, something about a business dinner. Jordan acted as though it didn't matter, but I saw a shadow flicker in his eyes as they walked away. We got drinks and carried on talking with lots of laughter. Nancy slipped her hand in mine, squeezing gently. Jordan and Lucy held hands and couldn't stop smiling at each other.

"Well done, Baby Girl. You've made us proud, hasn't she, Nancy?"

"Absolutely," Nancy agreed. "We're proud of both of you, especially for securing jobs in Birmingham."

Jordan's smile was genuine and broad. "Thanks, we can't wait to get started. Just need to find a place to rent now."

I frowned. "Isn't renting dead money?"

Jordan shrugged. "Maybe, but we all have to start somewhere, right Lucy?"

My Baby Girl nodded; her excitement palpable. "Exactly. Job, home, and whatever else comes along."

Nancy nudged me, her voice playful but with a knowing edge. "Well, we'd be happy to help you buy a house nearby, wouldn't we, Patrick?"

I grinned. "Only one daughter and we'd rather do it now while we're around to enjoy it."

Lucy's face lit up as she launched herself at me. "Mum, Dad, you're the best!"

"Calm down, Baby Girl," I chuckled. "We just want to see you more. It's all part of the plan." *Besides, I'm keeping hold of the deeds for now.*

Laughter filled the room, and in that moment, everything felt right. Family, love, happiness—it was all that mattered. I'd do anything for Nancy and Lucy. They were my world.

Jordan's family had given him a good start, but I offered more. I couldn't help but feel a bit smug about it. His parents might've set him up well, but I could provide them with a home. A house nearby meant I could keep Lucy close, safe. After everything that had happened, I wasn't ready to let her drift too far. It wasn't about control; it was about love. I needed to protect her, even if she didn't always see it. *Well, okay, maybe a little control. No harm in keeping an eye on her, right?*

The house we found in Earlswood was perfect. It needed work, but with Platt's Construction in my back pocket, nothing was impossible. As we walked through the house, Lucy and Jordan were already sketching out their dreams.

"I want this room knocked through," Lucy said, excitement bubbling in her voice. "Make it one big family room with views of the lakes."

Jordan grinned. "All I want is a den for myself. No girls allowed, right, Patrick?"

I laughed. "Sounds like you need a bar in there too. What do you say?"

Jordan's chest puffed out. "Now you're talking."

Lucy's eyes flickered with doubt as she looked at me. "Can we afford all this, Dad?"

"Nothing's too much for you, Baby Girl." I glanced at Nancy, who smiled in agreement.

"Sure is. We've come a long way from the shelter, haven't we, Lucy?"

Lucy's face scrunched up playfully. "Can't remember that far back, Mum!"

Nancy chuckled. "Guess so."

Lucy's whole demeanour softened. "Ted's the only thing I remember, and that's only because he's in every photo of me."

I smiled at the mention of Ted, her childhood toy, the second thing I ever bought her. "Ted's been with you through thick and thin. Don't let Jordan mess with him."

Jordan feigned a wince, his lip curling slightly. "Ted's the boss, I get it."

Nancy and I exchanged a look. Something about Jordan's reaction didn't sit right with me. A seed of doubt took root in my gut. A thousand little alarms went off inside, buzzing like an unstoppable swarm. From that moment on, I watched Jordan like a hawk, as vigilant as a guardian angel.

As the house transformed, we saw more of Lucy, but Jordan began to drift. He was always off to the gym, out drinking with mates, always rushing past us on his way out. The more absent he became, the more I determined to go around and visit on the pretence of different jobs. Work began to suffer, but my girl comes first.

"Sorry, Patrick, Nancy. Got to run. Next time, alright?"

Lucy made excuses for him, covering his absences with the same tired lines. It grated on me, but I bit my tongue.

Then one day, she started wearing baggy jumpers and oversized pyjamas, it was the last straw. "What's with the get-up, Lucy? It's only five in the afternoon."

Her smile faltered. "Just a bit under the weather, Dad."

Nancy, always the peacemaker, shot me a look. "Leave her be, Patrick."

Lucy forced a bright tone. "I'll make us all a cup of tea."

Something didn't sit right. No matter how hard I tried, I couldn't ignore the sense that things weren't as they seemed.

Nancy motioned for me to stay in the lounge as she slipped into the kitchen with Lucy. I hovered by the door, straining to catch their muffled words.

"Lucy, you've lost weight again. Are you alright?"

"Please, Mum, stop asking."

We hadn't planned to stay long. Lucy was a whirlwind—glowing one moment, her eyes wide and frantic, then scratching at her arms, glancing at the clock the next. Nancy caught my eye across the room, her quick nod barely perceptible, as Lucy looked away.

I pulled her into a hug, her frame fragile in my arms. "Baby Girl, what can we do to help?"

Her sobs tore through the silence, her body trembling as she pushed me away and collapsed into Nancy's embrace. She uttered words that broke my heart, her voice fragile, slicing through us. I handed her my handkerchief, crisp and white, watching her fingers cling to it. When her hand reached for mine, I grasped it like a lifeline, my own tears breaking free.

We listened as the words tumbled out—about Jordan, about the house, and how hard she tried to make things right. But the more she gave, the more distant he became. She lifted her sleeve, revealing purple marks staining her skin.

He hit my Baby Girl.

I twisted away, rage boiling over, and slammed my fist into the coffee table. Glass shattered, blood ran down my knuckles, shards scattering across the floor like a storm of tiny daggers.

Lucy recoiled, crawling into a corner, arms wrapped around her head.

"Lucy, love," Nancy's voice trembled, "Daddy's just angry at Jordan. Why don't you go and take a shower while we clear this up?"

Tears streaked her face as she nodded. "Alright, Mum. Are you sure you'll be okay?"

"We'll be fine, sweetheart. Your dad's just upset—at Jordan, not you."

"I'll be quick."

Nancy smiled softly. I looked down, shame gnawing at me. As soon as Lucy was gone, Nancy whisked me into the kitchen, the cold water biting as it seeped into the cuts. The pain was sharp, but nothing compared to the ache inside.

"Patrick, Lucy needs us now. This isn't the time to play the tough guy."

"I know, Nancy. I just can't stand him hurting her like this."

"He'll pay for it. I promise."

"This time… together."

We sealed it with a pinkie promise, like we did when we were young.

Lucy returned five minutes later all cleaned up. She sat gingerly on the sofa, her voice a notch above a whisper. "The first time Jordan hit me, he cried after, and things got better for a while. But then he started resenting my job, said it was getting in the way of our happiness. And he didn't like you both coming around so often."

"We're here because we love you," I said, my voice hoarse.

"I know, Dad. I know. But I quit my job two weeks ago. I thought it would make things better."

Nancy's face tightened. "But your job—you love it. And your friends…"

"I adore Jordan more," she said, her voice thin. "I'm trying to be a better partner for him."

"You'll miss it," Nancy said softly.

"You'll need money," I added, always practical. "You could work for me again. Do my books like you used to. I'll pay you well."

"You're the best parents anyone could ask for, you know that?" Lucy smiled, but it didn't reach her eyes.

Nancy and I exchanged a look. "Out with it," we said together.

Lucy chewed her lip, fingers twisting through her hair. "Could you ring before you come over? And maybe... just visit once a week, during the week?"

"Anything for you, Baby Girl."

That night, I hit the whiskey hard. One drink after another, trying to drown the anger clawing at me. After five shots, I grabbed my keys and headed for the car.

Nancy stepped in front of the door, appearing from nowhere. "You've had too much alcohol to drive."

"I need to go to the office." The usual code—I needed a thrill.

"If the police stop you, they'll take your licence."

I rested my hands on her shoulders, easing her aside. "I'm going to the office."

Driving away, I crushed the guilt beneath the wheel. I needed this. I'd earned it. Without it, I'd make Nancy's life worse than it had already become. The love of her life, Lucy, was falling apart—again. Our friends had stopped calling, and Nancy, too proud to reach out to them, stayed silent. My fault, I knew. But they didn't understand what weighed on me, or the secrets I carried.

*****

As the months passed, Jordan showed up less, which suited me just fine. But something about Lucy didn't add up. With her handling my books, I kept a closer eye, but the knot in my gut refused to loosen.

The day she telephoned because Jordan had locked her in the wardrobe was the worst day of my life. But seeing the strength in my girls that day—I was never prouder. And in that moment, I swore he'd pay for what he'd done.

Bad boys always get what's coming to them. Life has a way of seeing to that.

Chapter 10

Patrick—and the Medallion Man

DANIEL HAD THE WORK ethic, the looks, and a charm that drew people in, all wrapped in a cheeky smile. His roles as a rugby player and sports teacher gave him an easy confidence. There was much to admire, particularly his devotion to Lucy. But the numbers didn't add up—how could he afford a penthouse in Canary Wharf? A place like that must have cost a fortune. With a teacher's salary and Lucy pulling pints at a bar, it didn't make sense.

Lucy, though, acted like she'd hit the jackpot.

I pushed aside my doubts until they turned up at our place one weekend. Stepping out of his Range Rover Daniel tried to hide it, but he moved with such caution and stiffness I knew something was wrong. He cracked a joke to hide the tension.

I didn't laugh. "What happened to you?"

"Took a tumble at school. PE teacher's life, eh?" He winced, trying to flash that trademark smile.

"Looks like more than a tackle," I muttered, catching Nancy's warning glance.

Lucy crouched down, fussing over Rufus as if nothing had changed. "Hello, boy, still loving the attention, I see." She rubbed his belly, laughing.

Lucy waved Daniel closer. "Come meet Rufus."

We gathered around, and as I embraced my daughter, a promise stirred inside me—I'd get to the bottom of Daniel's act. Whatever had caused his 'tumble', at least Lucy had walked away unharmed.

The afternoon passed without incident, but then came the bombshell. As soon as I saw the trepidation on Lucy's face as they walked across the patio with the tea, I knew she was about to ask me something big.

Would I ever say no to my Baby Girl? Of course not. "Honestly, this house is empty without you."

"Champagne later, Patrick! Lucy and Daniel are moving to the Midlands!" Nancy beamed, her excitement making her bounce on the spot.

Lucy rushed over to me, not able to hide her excitement. "Dad, we can't wait to come home. It will be a fresh start for us. Thank you."

"We're thrilled to have you back, Baby Girl." I turned to Daniel. "Let's hope your move means fewer injuries, eh? Might be time to find a safer job, Daniel."

He grimaced through another forced smile, flashing a thumbs-up. With a smug look, he put an arm around Lucy. It was all part of his plan.

As soon as they settled, I went to the study. I picked up my mobile and dialled Sid's number. Shady, but he got results, more importantly he was a private investigator I trusted.

*****

In less than a week, he texted me: *Found something. Shall I come in?*

Text from Me: *Yes, tomorrow, 10 a.m. I need to hear what you've got.*

By the time Sid sat in my office, I was so worked up I couldn't stay still. He fumbled with his cup, rattling it in its saucer.

"For God's sake, get to the point. Put the damn tea down."

Tea sloshed over the sides as Sarah, my secretary, appeared. "I'll take that," she said, politely removing the cup from his shaky hands. "Anything else, Patrick?"

"We're fine. Thank you."

Sid wiped his forehead, his raincoat creaking as he slumped back onto the leather sofa. "You'd better sit down for this."

Swallowing hard I took a seat, dread making my hands clammy. Sid knew Lucy like family, understood how much she meant to me and what she'd been through.

Body language gives a lot away, and right then I knew how uneasy he was. "I've got bad news."

Using a rag, I wiped sweat off my forehead. "Get on with it, Sid. I can't stand the suspense."

Sid opened his notebook, glancing up occasionally as he read. "Daniel's dealing part-time. He's tied up with the Samuel Sampson gang and some Devon mob."

"No..."

"He got too cocky, dealt coke on Samuel's turf. Six weeks ago, they gave him a beating and told him to get out of London. Broke his arm and a few ribs, he's only just come out of the plaster cast. That's why they're moving up here."

I slammed my fist on the desk. "That's why he looked like that. We're bringing them here, and he's dragging trouble with him. God, he's a cocky bastard. And Lucy? Does she know?"

"She's involved, too, selling for him at the bar. She's discreet, but she's known."

I stared at him, my blood running cold. "Are you sure?"

"Here's a photo. She's sitting on one of those gold bar stools, dealing."

He handed me the picture. Lucy, clear as day, in new Gucci boots.

I pounded the desk again, my chest tight. "How did she meet him?"

"I guess she must have been lonely when she first moved to London. Met Daniel at a coffee shop... buying drugs."

Tears blurred my vision. "Why didn't she call me?"

Sid shook his head, his voice low. "I don't know, Patrick. It's a mystery."

I swallowed the tightness in my throat. "I've got to do something. Don't tell Nancy. She's thrilled about them moving to Lapworth, and she can't keep a secret from Lucy."

Sid leaned in. "What are you planning?"

I scribbled our home address on a scrap of paper, passing it across the desk. Sid took it without a word, slipping it into his coat. "In exchange for our safety."

"Say no more, Patrick. It'll be done."

The door clicked shut behind him, and I slumped at my desk, head in my hands. Everything hanging over me like a shroud, suffocating.

*****

Two weeks later, laughter and Rufus's barking filled the house as I stepped inside. The place felt alive again. Lucy had come home, and Daniel had started to grow on me—though knowing what I did about his dealings still ate away at me.

"Dad, we're in here!" Lucy's voice echoed from the living room. "Beating Mum at chess and teaching Daniel the rules."

I stepped in to see Daniel trying to defend himself. "Help me out, Dad—the girls are ruthless!"

Nancy chuckled, triumphant. "Oh, don't be such a sore loser, Daniel. Just because we're better."

Lucy blushed at his protest, while Nancy crossed her arms and jutted her chin at me, arching one eyebrow. I smiled, but I knew it didn't reach my eyes. *How can I tell her the truth?*

Sid had uncovered more. Daniel wasn't just dealing part-time, he was selling to schoolchildren, using Lucy's connections to expand. Worse, Lucy had become popular at the bar, but Sid warned something felt off. She'd gone from disliked to getting five-star reviews. I didn't want to believe it, but there it was.

Trying to keep up with the charade was exhausting. Then Daniel asked me for Lucy's hand in marriage.

I froze.

"Why don't you wait a bit?" I suggested. "Save some money. You've got years ahead, plenty of time."

"Dad, come on. When you know, you know. It's like a song you never get tired of hearing, a laugh you want to hear forever." Daniel's face was lit with conviction. "Tell me I'm wrong."

I sighed. "I get it. But think about the future—where you'll live, how you'll take care of Lucy."

Daniel smirked. "Bet you didn't think like that when you asked Mum."

He had me there. A reluctant smile crept across my face. "Fair enough. Ignore me. You've got my blessing."

Grinning, he slapped my back. "Thanks, Dad. I'll take her out for dinner, pop the question. I've already got the ring sorted. I'll hire a local trio to play something as I get down on one knee."

The memory of that same restaurant with Nancy brought a lump to my throat. "I'll give the Lapworth Trio a call and ask them to play *The Greatest Love of All* for you. That should bring the house down."

Daniel beamed. "You're the best. We'll celebrate with you when we get back. I'll bring something special for Rufus too."

As he left to get something from the car, my phone buzzed. Sid's name flashed on the screen.

"Patrick?" Sid's voice rasped through the line. "Are you ready?"

I hesitated, the room spinning around me. "Do it now."

The day blurred together. Nancy was giddy with excitement, planning a surprise party for the newly engaged couple, while Lucy floated around, high on love. Nothing could touch her—except I knew it was an illusion about to crash down on us all.

"Dad, we saw Uncle Sid today." Lucy's voice held a hint of curiosity. "He acted like he didn't recognise me."

My heart skipped. "Sid's always in a rush. I haven't seen him for a while either."

She ruffled Daniel's hair. "Yeah, he seemed busy."

After Lucy and Daniel left for their special night, spirals of self-doubt tightened the muscles in my chest until I clasped my chest in pain. Nancy babbled on about putting a bottle of fizz in the fridge, unaware of my mounting apprehension. Coming back from the kitchen five minutes later, she sighed and passed me a cup of tea.

"He's right for her, isn't he?"

I swallowed hard. "Time will tell."

"Wish we could be a fly on the wall when he proposes. Oh, I'm so excited for her. Do you think they'll have a white wedding?"

"Who knows, love?" We crossed our fingers, hoping for a perfect evening for them and settled in to watch TV while we waited for them to come home.

An hour later, the screech of brakes echoed on our drive, followed by a gunshot. The hairs on the back of my neck stood on end.

Nancy tensed beside me. "What was that? It sounded like a gun."

"Could be a car backfiring."

Ignoring me, Nancy shot towards the door. I beat her to it. "Stay here, I'll check it out."

After her nod, I reached for the door handle, only to hear her pick up the landline telephone.

Before I could tell her not to call the police, her eyes widened in fear, "It's dead! I'll get my mobile."

"Nancy, trust me. Let me check it out first." The stony look that suddenly came on her face showed me the penny had dropped and she realized that I knew what was going on. "I'll be right back."

I rushed to the back door where the shot had come from, body pumped with a rush of adrenalin. The shadows darting across the lawn made my blood run cold. Rufus lay in a pile of blood, whimpering. Tears blurred my vision as I knelt down beside him.

"There, boy." I stroked his head, voice cracking. "We love you."

He curled into a ball, his breath shallow. I knew it was the end. His death, sharp and unforgiving, felt like a knife to my chest. I could barely stand.

"Who are you?" Nancy's voice, sharp and defiant, broke through the haze.

Rushing back into the house, I found her bound on the sofa, being gagged by a man who stood over her, sneering.

Fury surged through me. "This wasn't part of the plan! Let her go. Rufus is dead—have you no decency?"

Nancy's eyes flashed with betrayal and my legs started to shake. "I was trying to protect Lucy." My words came out broken. "I'm sorry."

"Sit down and shut up." The short stocky Cockney, forced me onto the sofa. Using duct tape, he tied my ankles together and then my wrists behind my back. Nancy shrank away from me, her eyes filled with disbelief.

I couldn't stop them. I couldn't save Rufus. *What kind of protector am I?*

The tallest man came and knelt in front of me. "Your precious dog's gone now, Patrick. And soon, so will your prospective son-in-law. Steve owes me, and we're here to collect. Now where is he?"

A lump formed in my chest; rock hard, making breathing hard. *My god, Lucy, what if they hurt Lucy?* This was a nightmare of my own creation; one I was powerless to stop.

"Do I need to give you a bit of encouragement?" Under his balaclava the man in front of me moved his eyes from me to Nancy.

I shook my head. "They've gone out for dinner; they'll be back any moment now."

He reached out a hand and cupped Nancy's face. "Now that's better."

Get your hands off her! "We had a deal. Him for our safety."

As the man pulled back his hand, his sleeve rolled back revealing a tattoo of a snake eating a rat on his wrist. The image sent my panic level rising from a simmer to a full boil. Samuel Sampson had come in person instead of sending his henchmen. *This isn't good.* Sid had filled me in on this man's gory past.

"They won't be long, but please... please don't hurt our daughter."

The sparkle in his eyes filled me with dread as he stuck a piece of tape over my mouth. "I ain't a man who makes promises."

On the back of his threat, I spot Lucy peeking in the window. *Go, please, go. Run!* My Baby Girl disappeared and I hope she heard my silent plea.

"Let's do 'em in, guv," Cockney laughs.

Samuel scratches his woollen balaclava and I turn my head away as more of his face is revealed. "No need for that… just yet."

Cockney places the tip of his gun against the back of my head. "You sure, guv?"

A shot rings out and I lunge to the side to try and protect Nancy.

"That's a warning, now…"

Before Samuel can finish his sentence, a loud slam is heard from the kitchen.

Oh Lucy, Lucy… what are you doing?

*****

The police arrived the following morning, questions poured out, unrelenting. I told them everything. Lucy and Nancy looked at me with disbelief, but they couldn't argue with my loyalty.

In the end, the police caught Samuel Sampson and his gang. They didn't press charges against me or Lucy. I'd done all I could to save my family and although they didn't condone my actions, they understood them.

The National Drugs Intelligence Unit had been after the gang for a long time and using the information Sid and Lucy supplied, they were able to catch them red-handed in their next big delivery.

Because of this they decided to drop all charges against Lucy with a warning and a conditional stay in a rehabilitation centre.

She went into rehab, and six weeks later, my Baby Girl came home clean.

Chapter 11

Lucy—Aftermath

NO ONE EVER FOUND Daniel's body. Sometimes, I wondered if he was still out there dealing.

Every time a tall, broad-shouldered man of colour with gold jewellery caught my eye, memories of the 'Lapworth Trio' rushed back, along with the proposal—everything I'd wanted. The love of my life on one knee, the dining room falling into a hush as a waiter approached with a silver plate. A small box with a gleaming diamond nestled inside. And then every awful tiny bit of the evening would crash in on me and remind me how lucky I am that I never married him.

*****

While we waited for the police the day after the nightmare engagement, the memory of Daniel's pleas kept ringing in my ears as I remembered his desperate cries.

I was shaking like a leaf when they arrived. To them, it was a straightforward case; the infamous Samuel Sampson gang was a familiar enemy, and catching them in the act of their next pickup was their jackpot.

When my parents gave their version of events the truth struck me. Dad had hired Sid to dig into Daniel's past and had tipped off the gang about our location. Betrayal came like a punch to the gut and winded me.

As soon as the police car reversed out of the drive that day, I pounced on Dad. "Why didn't you tell me you knew about the drugs?" I punched the wall, the sharp pain detracting from the screaming rage rolling around in my head.

His voice heavy with regret, "I didn't want to believe you were involved. That snake took advantage of you."

"Dad, I'm not as innocent as you think. I wanted out of this conventional life." My heart raced, the awfulness of my past clawing at me.

"You're a good girl."

Cringing at the words, I forced myself to speak the truth. "No, no I'm not. I sold drugs in London and at Soogun."

He recoiled and for the first time in my life I thought he might hit me.

Mum reached out to soothe the air between us. "We can sort this out. Can't we, Patrick?" Mum's hope flickered in her eyes.

I could see the gears turning in Dad's mind. "We can try, Nancy, but Lucy, you have to get clean once and for all."

I nodded, running to him, my arms wrapping tightly around his waist. "I'm sorry for everything."

Mum came up behind me and joined in with a group hug. "We're so sorry, love. We know how much you cared for him."

Sniffling, I rubbed my eyes. "I did, but it wasn't meant to be. What are they going to do to him now?"

Dad's expression darkened. "I'm deeply sorry, Baby Girl. I thought they'd just scare him."

"They did that alright, but what about his sister?"

"Daniel was an only child."

I blinked, disbelief flooding me. "Are you sure, Dad? How could you know? The girlfriends at the rugby club said they'd met her… that she was nice."

"That's what Sid found out. Daniel used to belong to the Devon gang before he branched out with another dealer. It could be her they met, but it really doesn't matter does it? He's scum of the earth and probably every word out of his mouth was a lie."

My heart sank. "His whole life was a lie… how could I be so naïve? He claimed he was paying off his sister's debt to the gang and that they had videos of her to use against him."

"It's not your fault. He used you."

I pulled away from them. Heat rushed to my face, and I slammed my head against the wall, the physical pain needed to subdue the mental pain.

"Stop…" Mum coaxed me away from the wall to a seat on the other side of the table.

Dad's eyes brightened. I could see his determination. "Let's make a pact. What's done is done; we can't change the past, but we can change the future."

Mum clasped her hands. "How, Pat?"

"Tell me, Dad. What should we do?" I needed a plan, something to cling to.

"Let's learn from this." He pulled out a sheet of A4 paper and a pen. "We'll assign actions."

Mum exchanged a knowing look with me, and our feet touched under the table. Mum—my rock. I could do anything with her support. "Let's do this."

The first item was clear: 'Get Lucy clean.'

As I placed little packets of white powder on the table, fear coursed through me. This crutch, my confidence, my everything—it was all slipping away. I trembled, contemplating the life ahead of me, uncertain if I was ready to let go. Dad poured the powder down the sink. The rush of running water sounded refreshing. If there was a way forward, it depended heavily on my parents' support.

*****

The crunch of gravel under the tyres jostled my nerves, each road hump hitting harder than the last. Two hours of silence had passed between us, Dad gripping the wheel, eyes fixed on the endless motorway, black bags under his eyes and permanent crease marks in his forehead. He'd not had a drink since Daniel's abduction. I liked to believe that meant he suffered from guilt.

Mum hadn't come with us, this being too hard for her. *For her!* Over the last few days, she'd remained ashen under her blusher; every time I looked at her, guilt consumed me, so I was glad she wasn't there making the day all about herself. I cringed and pulled my cardigan tighter around me. *Where do these ugly thoughts come from?*

I stared out of the window, my mind swirling with dread. Mum had done my packing—gold chains, white cap, tracksuit, and Reeboks, all left behind. That life had been shed, like an old skin discarded for the start of something new.

We drove through a small town and as we came out of it we turned into a private drive. The car slowed as we approached the wrought iron gates, looming and foreboding. The sight of them sent a wave of cold panic through me. I glanced at Dad, the need for a hit rising like bile in my throat.

"Please… just one smoke. I know you've got something." My voice cracked, desperate.

Dad kept his eyes on the driveway. "No. Breathe. You'll be fine. It's just nerves."

"Don't tell me to breathe." I lashed out, a string of swear words tumbling out in quick succession. "You have no idea."

He smiled, the kind of smile that felt like a slap. "You'll fit right in."

I clenched my fists. "Give me something, Dad. I feel like I'm about to pass out."

"Look around." He nodded towards the parkland stretching beyond the hill. "You're lucky to be here. Look at that place—it's like a palace."

I grunted, anger rising. *Lucky?* Sure, if being 'lucky' meant pretending I wasn't craving a hit. Today I was meant to become someone new with a fresh start. No backstory, no past. Once I got clean, I'd be reborn. *Yeah, right!*

As we parked, music greeted us, the sound seeping through an open window, and for a moment, it softened the chaos inside me. A nurse in a white uniform approached, smiling like she already knew me. A porter grabbed my bags. The vibe too friendly, too relaxed. Yet it worked—my shoulders eased just a little as they welcomed me like an old friend.

I turned to Dad, hugging him, my voice breaking. "How did you manage this? You didn't give me anything, but I feel calmer. I'll make you proud, I promise Daddy."

A gentle mock-punch on my chin and his light-hearted grin reassured me, telling me how much he loved me more than words ever could. "You've always made me proud, Baby Girl. It's the people you choose that worry me."

Even then, he tried to make me laugh. I forced a smile, though it felt more like a grimace. "Where would I be without you?"

"Let's not think about that. Behave yourself. Listen. Share what you can. It's all confidential."

I love you so much, Dad. "I know." My gaze wandered, landing on a familiar face. "Wait—is that Ronnie Whitstone?"

The nurse chuckled. "Yes, but here, he's just Ronnie."

My mouth twitched in a smile. "Thanks."

She turned to me. "So, what do you want us to call you?"

"Lucy." I turned to Dad. "Six weeks. That's right, isn't it, Dad?"

His hand gripped mine, too tight, clammy. "Yes, six weeks. I'll come back for you."

The nurse held out her hand for my phone, laptop, anything else I might hide. Grumpy as hell, I dumped everything into her waiting hands. Dad drove away, waving, tears in his eyes. I stood there, empty, watching the car disappear down the gravel drive.

*****

The first meeting hit me like a tidal wave. Six people sat in a circle; eyes fixed on me the moment I entered. Perfect faces, clean clothes—none of them looked like junkies. The floor shifted beneath me as my nerves bubbled, I longed to make a bolt for the door.

One after the other, they started talking, spilling their truths.

A guy named David wore a ridiculous woolly hat, and I couldn't help but giggle as Jimmy cracked a joke. My turn came next, and I froze. Shrinking into myself, drowning in the silence… I needed a hit. Like right now.

"Uh… can I go tomorrow?"

Joe, the counsellor, nodded, his smile too kind. "Of course."

His warmth wrapped around me, like a flicker of life returning. I stole a glance—tall, athletic, blond hair that gave him a Viking-like appearance. Definitely someone I'd like to date. But I shoved the thought aside.

After the meeting, they introduced me to April, my Buddy. She'd been here longer and knew the ropes. I admired her honesty, though I remained wary. Who knew if she reported back to Joe?

We sat for coffee, chatting about activities.

Glancing over my shoulder, I leaned in, my lips inches from her ear. "Have you ever done coke?"

She nodded.

Speaking behind the veil of my hair, "Can you get me some?"

Her face hardened. "It's not that kind of place. We're here to get clean."

I crumbled. "Sorry. I don't have any willpower."

"Take this." She handed me a sweet. "Think happy thoughts."

Trying to stop my face from revealing my derision, I popped it into my mouth. *My dog died, in an awful way, that happy enough?*

Joe sat across the room, deep in conversation with another counsellor—a girl with a ponytail and porcelain skin. Not 'posh totty' like me, but she had that clean look, something untouchable. *The perfect girlfriend for a guy like Joe.* They seemed close.

April caught me staring. "That's Becky, Joe's girlfriend."

"Of course." Heat flushed my cheeks.

"He's dreamy, isn't he? Got a great personality too. He makes me laugh all the time. They're both counsellors and they've been living together a while now," she added, voice low. "Not that anyone understands why. She's… well, different." April put her hands over her mouth to whisper. "You don't want to get on the wrong side of her."

"She looks familiar to me."

"Apparently, she came here from London and back in the day she was a free spirit. Rumour is she came here on the run from some bad relationship breakup. But honestly no one knows for sure and well… who cares?"

I jumped when they walked over and knocked over my cup which thankfully was nearly empty. I swiped at the dripping coffee with a serviette.

Joe smiled. "Lucy, this is Becky. She'll be working with you too."

Becky's eyes met mine. "I think we've met before, years ago."

"I thought the same," I said, casting a glance at April, who nodded in agreement.

"Well, I'm sure we'll get to know each other better over the next six weeks." Becky's tone was sweet but edged with something sharp.

April and I wandered into the library where the others sat, exchanging stories, their faces animated in the dim light.

"Didn't you do enough of that earlier with Joe?"

David, the lanky guy with his ever-present, brightly coloured woolly hat glanced our way. "This is different. We're sharing because we want to, not because we have to."

"Come on, Lucy Loo, what's your story?" Jimmy, the joker of the group, grinned at me.

"Alright, you've got me. Where do I start? Maybe the part where I'm a sex slave to a famous actor," I teased, locking eyes with him.

Jimmy's grin widened. "Now we're talking! Spill it, Lucy. Something spicy and hot!" His tongue nearly hung out as the others leaned in.

"Well, let's call him Richard. He liked his privacy. The first time he clocked eyes on me, I was singing in a school play. Afterward, he met my parents, offering to be my voice coach—free of charge." My voice quivered slightly as they sat transfixed on me.

"Oh God, I know where this is going," Jimmy muttered, only to get smacked on the head by David. "Lucy, keep going."

“My mum dropped me off at his studio every week, probably grabbed a coffee at a nearby café, maybe even a cake.” I smirked, playing with the tension in the room.

I hadn’t noticed Joe slip in, quietly taking a seat.

Jimmy’s voice cut in. “Come on, we’re on the edge here!”

“My singing improved, along with my… knowledge of how to please a man.” I fluttered my eyelashes, enjoying their attention, the teasing hint in my voice drawing them in further.

“What did he want?” Jimmy’s hand scribbled furiously in his notebook.

“He made me read stories and act them out. You know, the type they sell in brown paper bags at newsagents.” Their eyes widened, silence swallowing the room.

Jimmy sat on the edge of his seat. “What was the magazine? ‘Slut’? ‘GQ’? ‘Rider’? Come on, Lucy, tell us,”

I held their gaze a second longer before bursting into laughter. “It was ‘The Beano.’ Dennis the Menace was his favourite.”

The group erupted into gasps, then laughter, as Jimmy threw his hands in the air.

David smirked, shaking his head. “Good one, Lucy. We’ll get you back for that!” I grinned back at him and we shared a moment of camaraderie and I knew then we’d always look out for each other.

“You’re a tease!” Jimmy stormed out of the room, slamming the door behind him, but the slow clapping from the back drew all attention.

Joe stood, the room falling silent. “Well, Lucy, the actress. You’re good. Tomorrow morning, let’s hear the real story. I’m looking forward to it.” With giving me a chance to answer, he left the room.

"You'll be in trouble…" April leaned close, her breath tickling my ear, "if Becky finds out Joe fancies you."

"No, he doesn't!" But a tingle ran through me, heat rising in my cheeks as I crossed my fingers. When I realized what I'd done, I shook my hands. *Silly childish habit. Luck is non-existent in my life.*

Lights-out came at 11pm. Restless and anxious, I tossed in bed, my mind spinning. Soon, Joe and I would meet one-on-one to sort out a treatment plan. Funny how I didn't think I needed a plan. I only did coke two, maybe three times a week. But I'd promised Mum and Dad. I couldn't let them down.

At 3am I got out of bed and paced. *I'm not an addict! I shouldn't be here.* But I craved a fix. My skin felt too tight, my chest heavy, and an odd itch spread through my veins, like my blood wanted to jump out of my skin. My mind needed something to calm my stress, but that's all cocaine was to me, I wasn't hooked on it.

*****

The next morning, I showered early, letting the hot water flow over me as I scrubbed every inch, making sure I looked my best for Joe. One addiction had already shifted to another, but this one had a face and body to match. The image of Becky's face hovered before me, I stuck my tongue out. *All's fair in love and war, right?*

I arrived last, slipping into the only open seat, directly across from Joe. No chance to hide. My stomach twisted; the room hummed with anticipation.

"So, Lucy," Joe smiled broadly, "ready to share your story?"

"Yes, okay." I took a deep breath, my heart racing. "I'm here because I started using cocaine in London and it gave me confidence… or at least I thought it did. I want to get clean, go back home to my parents. They're in the Midlands, and they deserve better from me. I've heard that these group sessions can help me change the way I think and act."

The room stayed quiet, all eyes on me as I continued.

"My dealer in London was Daniel. Gorgeous, muscular, a PE teacher at a local school. We met at a coffee shop, and it was lust at first sight. Before long, I started selling coke too—through my job at a bar in Canary Wharf. We had it all. Friends, money, the lifestyle. It felt like a dream."

Joe nodded, his eyes holding mine, urging me to keep going.

"Daniel and I… we were everything to each other. But after he got beaten up, we left London. Moved to my parents' place. They welcomed him like family." I paused, my throat tightening. "But it wasn't enough for Daniel. He convinced me to start dealing again. We hid it from my family. They'd have kicked us out if they knew."

I hesitated, swallowing the knot in my throat. "It wasn't until later I realised… Daniel wasn't who I thought he was. He was a thug, a dealer. I'd brought danger into my parent's house."

A gasp escaped April's lips, but Joe motioned for silence.

"What happened to Daniel?" Joe's voice remained soft but steady.

"We don't know," I admitted. "One day, a gang took him. I think… he might be… dead." The words left my mouth, hollow and final, and I stared ahead, empty.

Joe, genuine sympathy oozing from him, leaned forward. "I'm so sorry, Lucy."

"I… I need a break." I buried my face in my hands.

The group gathered around me, offering biscuits, water, comfort. For a moment, we were bonded—not by our stories but by our shared addiction, the elephant in the room none of us could ignore.

*****

Two days later, I sat across from Joe for our one-on-one. Something about him made it easy to open up. He didn't push or judge, just listened like my future actually mattered to him. After talking through the plan, we both signed off on it, and he handed me medication to help me sleep. Ironically, he warned me not to take too much, in case I developed a dependency. Funny how that worked—trading one addiction for another.

The next day, I had my first session with Becky. Her sweet smiles and soft voice felt almost too comforting, like she was trying a little too hard. Something about her was off. Her voice tugged at a memory, a distant echo I couldn't place. The London accent might've masked it, but I could tell we had crossed paths before.

"Becky, have you ever lived in the Midlands?"

She nodded. "Yes, I was born there. Moved back again for a couple of months before I went to London. That's when I started counselling, got this job at The Hedgeway, and met Joe. Why?"

I studied her, trying to piece it together. "You look familiar. Maybe you've got a doppelgänger running around."

She laughed, but something flickered in her eyes. "Could be. Or maybe we did meet, a long time ago. I went to St. James School in Lapworth for a bit when I was a kid."

The name clicked, but I couldn't fully recall. "I don't remember you."

"I wasn't there long. My first adoptive parents split up, sent me back to the orphanage, and I was adopted again not long after. Ended up at St. James halfway through the term."

My mind scrambled, pulling fragments of a past I'd tried to forget. "Maybe you looked different then... did you know a guy named Jeff? Played the guitar?"

Her smile faltered. "Yes, I did. We lived together in this disused railway station for a while. Then one day, he just disappeared."

My pulse quickened. "I thought you both went to London?"

Recognition dawned on her face. "Wait, you're Lucy, aren't you?"

Heat rose to my face as I locked eyes with her. "Yeah. And you're the one who took Jeff from me."

Her expression hardened. "According to Jeff, you were just mates. He said your parents were letting him crash there."

I clenched my fists, my thoughts racing back to the lies Jeff had spun. "Jeff was never honest about anything. But if he didn't leave with you, and he didn't come home to me... where did he go?"

Becky shrugged, got up and began pacing the room. "I don't know, and I don't care. He wasn't worthy of either of us."

I stared at her, disbelief curling through me. "I tried to find him after you left. The others told me you both went to London. You're sure he didn't go with you?"

Her arms flung out in exasperation. "I think I would've noticed if he came with me."

I needed answers. "Can I borrow your phone? You know we're not allowed to have ours in here, and I need to call my dad."

Becky hesitated, then pulled out her phone, glancing around before slipping it to me. "Be careful. If anyone sees, I could lose my job."

I nodded, taking it from her. Outside, I dialled Dad's number. It rang, and then his familiar voice came through, warm and surprised. "Hello, can I help you?"

"Dad, it's me. Lucy."

His tone shifted to concern. "You alright, Baby Girl?"

"I'm fine, Dad. I just wanted to check in."

I could almost hear him thinking, piecing together how to answer. "We're fine. Counting the days until you can come home. How are things there?"

"Good. Joe's been amazing. He's got me to share my story with the group. It's gruelling, but... he makes it easier."

Dad's voice softened, pride edging through. "That's great, love. Your mum will be thrilled when I tell her."

"Dad, you'll never guess who works here."

He sounded curious. "Who?"

"Becky... from the railway station, the one Jeff hung out with."

There was a pause, before an intake of breath. "I remember her. She met Jeff when I dropped him off."

"You never mentioned that before." Suspicion laced my words.

"I didn't want to upset you, especially after the *accident*."

"She told me Jeff didn't come back that night, after he'd done a job for you."

Dad's tone grew tight, defensive. "I dropped him there. Becky was waiting. I don't know anything else."

Something didn't add up. "Dad... are you sure?"

"I'm sure. Can we talk about something else now? I don't have much time."

"Alright. How's Mum?"

He chuckled. "Busy making sweets. Says they're for when you come back, and I'm not allowed to touch them. The smell of fudge is driving me nuts!"

I forced a laugh, but as the call ended, doubts swamped me. What would Becky have to gain from lying? But Dad... *he* was hiding something.

Chapter 12

Lucy—Irresistible Pull

DURING MY STAY, Jo treated me kindly, but over the last five weeks, a shift had crept in. He avoided eye contact, kept things strictly professional, distant even, as if there was a barrier between us that hadn't been there before.

Moved permanently to Becky's group, part of me wondered if paranoia was a side effect of the withdrawal—because I felt betrayed, like I'd been dumped. Something had shifted, and the only reason possible was that I'd upset him. Maybe I'd shared too much, made a fool of myself. The more I thought about it, the worse I got, regret eating at me.

I missed the old group, missed the easy banter with David and Jimmy. I still saw April in the evenings, but it wasn't the same. Now, it was just Becky and a bunch of strangers in the group sessions. I couldn't help but feel out of place, awkward, and exposed. I rambled on during the sessions, spilling my thoughts carelessly, the words slipping from my mouth before I could catch them. Shame burned in me, and I wished I could disappear, wished the floor would swallow me up whole.

Joe didn't accept a cup of coffee from me anymore. If he saw me coming down the hall, he turned the other way. I couldn't understand why he had pulled back so harshly. Was it me? Had I said too much? Had the real me repulsed him? I slumped into a chair, head in my hands, rocking slowly. I fancied him, there was no denying that now. The attraction had grown, deepened in ways I hadn't expected, and admitting it to myself felt like a mistake I couldn't take back.

It had been only two months since Daniel proposed and I'd thought all my dreams had come true. It was pure craziness to find myself falling for someone new so soon, but I couldn't deny my growing affection.

Becky was different now. Gone was the salacious hippy I'd first met at the station, the one whose free-spirited, almost reckless energy had made me keep my distance. I'd judged her then—bright clothes, big laugh, always with that edge of flirtation—but now, she'd become like the sister I never knew I needed. She'd surprised me, revealing a depth I hadn't expected, always there, always listening with that calm, steady presence.

But there were fleeting moments where her gaze lingered a beat too long, or she asked questions that dug deep, like she needed to pull at something inside me. I brushed it off, thinking I was paranoid, still shaken from everything I'd been through. After all, she'd been peeling back my layers, one by one, and though it hurt, I needed to go through this process. There was so much about myself I hadn't wanted to face and still much I needed to change.

Despite the mess in my head, group work had its moments of lightness, almost like it wasn't rehab at all. Yet, every time I thought of Joe, my chest tightened. It hurt in a way I didn't want to admit. I caught myself watching him too closely, my heart stumbling whenever Becky flashed him a smile.

She radiated joy, spinning in her bright green top and yellow trousers, playful and carefree. I hated how beautiful she was; how natural their connection appeared to be. Joe, with his film-star looks, couldn't take his eyes off her. He kissed her on the lips, right there in front of everyone, and jealousy sank deep in my gut. I loathed myself for it. She had only ever been kind to me since I arrived.

That afternoon, I avoided Joe before he could shun me, and ducked into a side corridor when I saw him coming. But his voice caught me.

"Lucy, wait."

I turned slowly; my words sharp before I could stop them. "Oh, you're talking to me now?"

He hesitated, shuffling on his feet. "I don't know what you mean."

"Sure you do." I glanced at my watch to hide the sting of rejection.

"Do you have somewhere to be?"

"No, but I don't have time for your mixed signals, Joe. I've got a life to get back to in a couple of weeks."

He looked caught off guard, like he hadn't expected me to be so blunt. "I thought we had more time."

"More time for what? Watching paint dry?"

He paced, hands twisting nervously. "I'm with Becky, you know that. And professionally, I can't date a patient. That's why I moved you to her group. I didn't want to... back off completely."

His words hit me hard. I stood there, close to heartbreak, but I masked it with a shrug. "Good excuse."

Joe reached out, catching my hand, his eyes searching mine. "Let me explain. Come for a coffee with me… outside."

Unsure, but wanting more than anything to be with him, I nodded. He took my hand, and for a moment, I let myself be pulled along, a mix of guilt and longing tangling inside me. We dashed through the corridors like school kids, throwing open the doors and breathing in the fresh air, laughing too loudly, too freely.

I glanced at him, feeling reckless. "Let's climb the wall and head to the café across the road. I saw it when Dad dropped me off."

He laughed, shaking his head but mounting the wall anyway. "You're a troublemaker, Lucy."

I blushed, suddenly self-conscious as I scrambled up after him, my skirt riding high. My cheeks burned as I remembered what I was wearing underneath—too little for a moment like this.

"Come on, jump!" On the other side of the wall, Joe stretched out his arms, his eyes glinting with mischief.

I landed awkwardly, brushing off the dirt as I stood up. We walked together to the café, the rush of the outside world hitting me like a wave. Buses screeched by, people hurried past, and for a moment, it felt like I was part of it again. Like I wasn't trapped in some facility, waiting for my life to restart.

A rebellious spirit thrilled me. A buzz because we had stepped outside the rules. If we got caught, I knew I'd shoulder the blame. They'd expect it of me, not Joe—he had his polished image, the professional who could do no wrong. He had a lot to lose—and that enhanced every emotion of longing for him I had.

As we walked in, an older couple, matching lime green jumpers and all, stared at us over their lattes. Cupped hands over their mouth didn't hide their snide comments. Their eyes gleamed with the kind of mischief only nosy onlookers could muster.

The café hummed with life, nearly every table filled, but we found a perfect spot at the front in a window seat, overlooking the road. As I sat down across from Joe, I couldn't help but think how normal it all seemed. But deep down, I knew the truth. I had a lot to face when I left The Hedgeway. A lot to fix, inside and out. And Joe? He was just a piece of that puzzle, nothing more. At least, that's what I kept telling myself.

Mr Green Jumper leered at me until my face burned—bright as my red underwear—knowing he must have watched my awkward scramble over the wall. When they stood up to leave, I was relieved but then he had the nerve to wink at me and drop his card on the table.

"You'd be lucky." I tossed it to the floor. "And I'd have to be desperate!"

Joe glanced over. "What was that?"

"Just some pervy voyeurs with nothing better to do."

As they scurried out, the man circled back to grab his card, shooting me a final jab. "Your loss."

I held my nose and grinned. "No doubt some lucky girl will get the chance of a lifetime. Hope you both enjoy it!" He stormed off, and his wife smacked him with her handbag, their bickering echoing as they disappeared down Victoria Street.

I looked at Joe, who was shaking with laughter. "There's never a dull moment with you."

I couldn't help but laugh too, the tension breaking as we scanned the menu.

"What'll it be, Lucy?"

"An extra hot latte sounds amazing."

Sitting there, the sun streaming through the window, the oak trees swaying outside, and The Hedgeway's brick walls in the distance, I received a strange comfort. It reminded me of home, though a part of me longed for Mum and Dad. The rush of buses and cars on the street tugged at something deep inside me—the world I'd left behind. It startled me how quickly I'd adapted to the routine, the confines of the place, even though it felt like a holding pattern.

I needed my life back.

But with Joe sitting across from me, the thought of leaving felt impossible. *How could I walk away from him?*

I had to be smart. This was my chance to change, to grab hold of the things I was learning here. I needed to face my weaknesses—men, loneliness, the danger they carried. When I left, I'd find someone different, someone who didn't come with drugs or chaos. Joe was just a distraction, wasn't he? Something to pass the time until I left this place.

“This,” I gestured at the café around us, “is exactly what I needed. A glimpse of what I’ve been missing.”

Joe’s smile wavered, his gaze dropping. “I get that. But it hasn’t all been bad, has it?”

“No, meeting you was the best part. Though you’ve blanked me for weeks. Why?”

His fingers fidgeted on the table. “Becky needs me. She’s been through a lot.”

“She seems confident. Like nothing could touch her.”

Joe shook his head. “Not at all. She’s had a tough life.”

I reached across the table, taking his hand. “Tell me.”

He hesitated, then spoke quietly. “You can’t repeat this—I’d be fired on the spot.”

“I won’t. You have my word, besides I think I already know a lot of what you’re going to say.”

Joe blinked, surprised.

“When we realized we’d met before, we had a small conversation, but go ahead and share with me because I want to understand.”

“Her mum died when she was young. Her dad didn’t want her, so she ended up in care, where things... weren’t good. She was adopted twice, but the second set of parents turned out to be very strict, and she ran away at fourteen. Lived on the streets for a while.”

I could feel a lump forming in my throat. “I didn’t know. She’s come so far.”

“She has. Spent time moving around, squatted in a disused railway station once before she decided to turn her life around.”

Every word highlighted the worst in me. *I’m such an awful person.* “No wonder you love her.”

Joe squeezed my hand, the warmth of his skin making something inside me stir. I glanced up, meeting his gaze, and for a moment, everything else disappeared. His eyes softened, and I saw it—a flicker of something unspoken. The space between us hummed with tension, not the uncomfortable kind, but the kind that felt like a quiet understanding. It was as if, without a word, we both acknowledged what had been simmering beneath the surface all along.

A jolt shot through me, like fireworks bursting behind my eyelids, the intensity catching me off guard. The realisation of what this moment meant settled in, sending tears trickling down my cheeks.

"What's wrong?"

"Nothing." I tilted my head towards him, my gaze unwavering and my voice soft. "I'm just... happy. I can't believe this."

It wasn't the words that passed between us—it was the recognition in his eyes, the same longing reflected back at me. The silent admission that we both wanted this, whatever 'this' was. A rush of emotions surged through me, and I knew that, for now, we were on the same page, both daring to cross a line neither of us could deny any longer.

Joe walked around the table and kissed me on the cheek, blissfully unaware of the people outside looking in. He squeezed my hand, and we fell into an easy rhythm, words tumbling between us as if we'd known each other forever. The café buzzed around us, but it felt distant, like white noise.

I didn't notice Becky until her voice cut through the warmth between us.

"Well, Joe, surely I deserve an explanation?"

Her presence sent a chill through the air. Joe stiffened beside me, his smile fading as he turned to face her.

"Hello, Becky," he said, trying for casual, but the tension in his voice betrayed him. "I'm just having a coffee with Lucy."

Becky's gaze darted between us, sharp, assessing. "A bit more than a coffee, from what I can see." Sarcasm dripped from her words.

I forced a smile, hoping to diffuse the situation. "It's rehab, Becky. Joe had some free time, so we're grabbing a coffee. Nothing more."

"Rehab, right. Not exactly by the book, though, is it, Joe?" Becky's tone hardened. "Maybe I should call it in."

Joe's hand tightened around mine. "Becky, don't."

Ignoring him, Becky fumbled in her bag. "I'll just take a few pictures on my way out, then." Her voice cracked, the bitterness not masking her hurt.

Before either of us could respond, Becky stumbled back, her distress obvious. She knocked into a chair, arms flailing as the café owner hurried over, ushering her outside.

"Sorry, love," he said, passing her a tissue. "No photos allowed in here. There's a sign."

Becky didn't argue. She stood there, dabbing at her eyes, pointing towards Joe with trembling fingers. "But we love each other. We were making plans…"

The café fell silent. The sound of horns blaring outside cut through the moment as Becky crossed the road without looking, narrowly avoiding a collision.

I turned to Joe; my voice low. "Shouldn't you go after her?"

His expression darkened. "No point. She'll tell everyone anyway. Cry, make me the villain. Might as well stay away."

Condemnation swirled from glance to another, making me feel exposed, like we were on display. "Let's just go."

Joe nodded, standing quickly. I grabbed my bag, nearly knocking over my chair in the process. The café owner offered a sympathetic smile as we left, but it did nothing to ease the knot tightening in my chest.

Once outside, Joe squeezed my hand again, pulling me into the cool air. "I thought you had a meeting?"

"I'm not going. Becky will have told everyone about us. I'm going to be the villain in the play, that's for sure. What are you going to do?"

"My time here is done. I need to face the music but there's no way they will keep me on now."

"Why don't you call in sick? Give yourself some time to think it through."

He let out a hollow laugh, but his eyes had lost their light. "Let's just have fun, okay? Worry later."

His carefree tone didn't match the unease settling in my gut, but I agreed and holding hands we went for a long walk and talked for hours.

When we returned, Becky was waiting, her face a mask of disappointment. "You missed your counselling session." With her foot tapping, she folded her arms. "Is that how you treat someone who listens to you? Who's supposed to be your friend?"

I looked down at my feet, unable to meet her gaze. "I'm sorry, Becky. I truly am." And I was. I sort of hated myself in that moment. I wished with all my heart that Joe had been single and I hadn't hurt her.

"Be sorry later." From the tip of my dark roots to my toes curled in my shoes, her icy glance judged me. "We've got a one-on-one session after dinner. Don't forget."

Joe came to my room just before dinner, looking worse for wear—his face pale, dark stubble shadowing his jaw. "I love you," he murmured, the words heavy in the quiet room.

I tried to muster enthusiasm, but his exhaustion mirrored my own. "Me too, and I don't want to leave you."

"I've been sacked," Joe admitted, sinking onto the bed. "Becky threw my clothes out of the window. I had to pick them up off the ground."

The image of him, scouring the dirt for his belongings, made my heart ache. "Come back with me," I blurted. "Mum and Dad will love you. There are other jobs. We'll figure it out."

Joe's eyes flickered with a hint of hope. "Are you sure?"

I nodded, my chest tightening. "I'll call Mum." I rushed to reception and requested my phone. I'd already asked them to make arrangements for me to leave so the woman behind the desk handed it over.

Back in the room, I fumbled with my phone and dialled Mum's number. After a few rings, she answered the video call.

"Hello, Darling, how are you?" Her voice was bright, oblivious to the storm brewing around me.

"Good, Mum, can't wait to see you tomorrow. Is Dad coming to pick me up?"

There was a pause. "Yes… is everything alright? We just got the call that you're ready to leave early. Are you sure that's a good thing?"

"Yes, Mum, I do. I'm good, really good. I've got a friend coming home with me. I'd like them to stay a while, is that's okay with you and Dad?"

"A friend?" Mum sounded puzzled. "Do we know her?"

"It's a guy, Mum. Joe. He works here… and, well, we've fallen for each other."

I glanced at Joe, catching the blush creeping up his neck. I smiled, trying to lighten the mood.

Mum's breath caught on the other end of the line. "Will he be in the spare room?"

I couldn't help but laugh. "No, Mum. He'll be in my room."

Joe stifled a cough.

Not wanting to give Mum the chance to refuse I finished the call. "See you tomorrow, Mum. Love you."

As I hung up, I turned to Joe, grinning. "You should've seen her face."

Joe shook his head, smiling despite himself. "Isn't this a bit fast?"

I shrugged, blinking back sudden tears. "Not for me."

Joe pulled me close, wrapping me in his arms. "It's what I want too, but… how's your dad going to take this?"

"Dad only wants what's best for me." I leaned into him. "And that's you."

Joe's grin widened. "We'll finish this conversation later. For now, you've got dinner and a lot of gossip to deal with."

I laughed, grabbing his hand. "I'll bring you a doggy bag." Then, with a sigh, I added, "And I've got my last one-on-one with Becky. That'll be fun."

Joe's expression darkened, but he squeezed my hand, letting me go. "Maybe you should cancel it."

"The receptionist told me I need a counsellor to sign me off, and as that can't be you…"

Truthfully, I dreaded the meeting, but I was done with hiding and fear. These last four weeks had taught me that I needed to stand up for myself and speak my mind instead of bottling it all inside. Even if facing Becky filled me with dread, I knew I couldn't keep running from what scared me.

Chapter 13

Lucy—Fractured Ties

BECKY STORMED into the room, slamming the door behind her. "Well, I didn't see that coming, Lucy! I really underestimated you."

I sat hunched, head in my hands. "Becky, it wasn't planned. We love each other. I never meant to hurt you. I like you, and I hope we can get past this." I couldn't see that happening, but I had to try.

She stared at me, her words dripping with venom. "Oh, you'll both be sorry. Trust me. I've got something special lined up for Joe. Can't wait to see how he talks his way out of this one."

My brow furrowed, a knot tightening in my chest. "What do you mean?"

Becky smiled coldly. "No need to worry. It's all for Joe. Should be fun to watch."

Anger surged through me. "Don't act so high and mighty, Becky. You stole Jeff from me back in Lapworth. Don't think I've forgotten."

She dismissed it with a wave as she sat in the chair opposite me. "We've been over this. He told me you were just a friend. Jeff didn't turn up the night I left—he had to handle some urgent job for your dad."

"Convenient excuse, wasn't it? He saw through you, didn't he?"

"No. I waited for him, but then I left for London. Jeff was a loser anyway. You should thank me. If you knew the things he said about you…huh!"

Really? With a scowl I slumped back against the couch. "Are we going to do this one-to-one or not?" *Why on earth did I come?*

Becky dragged her chair a bit closer. "If we have to." She got straight to the point. "So, what have you learned about yourself while you've been here?" She flipped open her file on me and turned to a blank page.

Why am I here? I'll never get her to see how sorry I am. This is a waste of time. "I've learnt a lot... but nothing I want to share with you." I rose slowly, turning back just as I reached the door. Becky stood up; her eyes cold, hollow. A chill ran through me, sharp as a blade.

If you could kill me you wouldn't hesitate, would you? I slipped outside shutting the door quietly behind me.

I was surprised to find Joe waited for me. He took one look at my face and pulled me in close.

"Aaaaarrrhhhh!" The scream came from inside Becky's office. It sounded like something out of a nightmare—high, shrill, and full of pain. I cringed, shutting my eyes against the pain it transmitted through the door.

"What the hell was that?" Joe's voice cracked with panic and his face paled visibly.

My stomach cramped, goosebumps breaking out on my skin. "It's Becky... What should we do?"

Ben darted past us, racing into the room. We watched as he pulled Becky into his arms, holding her tight until her screaming slowed to sobs. He passed her tissues, rocking her like a child before yelling at us to close the door.

Joe tugged at my arm. "Let's go, Lucy. There's nothing more we can do here. Ben will take good care of her."

I nodded. "I feel terrible."

Back in my room, the tension hung heavy between us. We climbed into bed, spooning silently, hands linked but minds elsewhere. Tomorrow, we would leave this place behind. But nothing felt settled.

I couldn't shake the increasing fear that everything I'd built over the last five weeks—every step towards healing—could unravel in an instant. What if our future together was cursed before it even began? We were starting this chapter based on someone else's pain, and the thought of it didn't sit well with me. Was this how bad karma took root? Was I dooming us before we had a chance? The idea of building a life on the wreckage of Becky's heartbreak felt like a stain that no amount of love could wash away.

And yet… every relationship I'd had until now had been tainted from the start—hidden lies, unspoken betrayals, cracks beneath the surface that I'd always been too hopeful to see. Each one had crumbled, but I'd clung on, convincing myself that things could change. This time felt different. With Joe, I let myself believe I'd found something real, something that could last. It felt good at its core—honest, without the shadows that had always haunted my past. For once, I wasn't chasing a dream. I thought I'd finally caught it.

*****

No one came to see us off. Not even the friends I'd made. It didn't matter. We'd broken an unspoken rule, and now everyone would side with Becky. She and Joe had been the golden couple—the ones everyone loved. And me? I was just the druggie who'd waltzed in, stirred the pot, and left with the prize.

Dad was waiting on the drive for me as we came out. I flung my arms around him. "It's so good to see you!"

"You too, Baby Girl." He turned to Joe, giving him a once-over. "So, you're Joe? The guy Mum's told me about."

Joe reached out, offering a nervous handshake. "Hello, Patrick. Thank you for having me. I hope it won't be for long, just until I find a new job. I want you to know that I appreciate this a lot."

Dad grinned, giving Joe's hand a firm shake. "No problem. Any friend of my daughter is welcome. Isn't that right, Lucy?"

I smiled, a surge of warmth washing over me. "Absolutely, Dad."

The ride home passed in quiet conversation, the countryside rolling by in soft greens and golds. Dad kept the mood light, mentioning Mum's fresh haircut and how proud she'd be to show it off. "Don't forget to tell her you noticed, Joe."

Joe gave a grateful smile. "Thanks for the heads-up."

The drive continued with little more than the occasional remark about lambs or cows in the fields. Then, as we finally pulled up to the house, Joe squeezed my hand. His touch sent a warm wave through me, and for a moment, I let myself believe everything might turn out alright.

Mum burst out of the door before Dad had parked, running toward me with open arms. We collided, laughing and crying all at once.

I glanced over my shoulder, spotting Joe standing awkwardly by the car, his eyes wandering as though unsure where he stood in that moment.

"Joe, come and meet Mum!" I beckoned him over.

Mum's eyes lit up when she saw him. "Wow! Don't you make a handsome pair!"

I chuckled. "Told you, he's perfect."

Dad clapped Joe on the shoulder. "Come on in, lad. We'll get your stuff settled, then maybe grab a beer. These two will be chatting for hours, so we might as well make ourselves comfortable."

Joe looked relieved. "Beer sounds great, thanks."

Mum pulled me aside for a quick moment, her eyes scanning me with motherly concern. "You're glowing, Lucy. This Joe, he's the real deal, isn't he?"

I smiled. "He is. What do you think of him?"

"He's not your usual type, with those big eyes and fair hair."

"I know, but he's a keeper." I rubbed my clammy hands on my dress.

Mum's smile faltered, replaced with a look of concern. "He worked at The Hedgeway?"

"Yeah, but he left to come back with me."

"Why not just take a holiday?"

"He used to be with another counsellor, Becky. It got... complicated."

Mum raised an eyebrow. "So, you're the other woman?"

I bristled. "Mum, be happy for me. He's perfect. Let's go inside so you can get to know him properly."

Inside, Dad and Joe were already laughing over beers, their earlier awkwardness gone. The sight of them like that warmed my heart. Maybe this was the fresh start I needed.

But in the back of my mind, a small voice whispered: *What if it all goes wrong?*

*****

Joe landed a job within weeks, and it paid more than The Hedgeway. A solid nine-to-five. A true victory.

I joined Dad at Platt's Construction straight away and realised that the years spent watching him work had given me a deeper knowledge than I'd thought. I wasn't just doing the books; I understood the business. As the weeks rolled by, I grew in confidence and happiness bubbled inside me all the time. *How did I get so lucky?*

One day, Dad looked at me, pride swelling behind his words. "You were always meant to be here. At least now I know I'll leave this place in safe hands when my time comes."

"Don't say that, Dad." The thought of losing him hurt too much. "I can't imagine this place without you."

"You're one of the guys now. They trust you, Lucy. What more could a father ask for?" His chest puffed out as he struggled with a laugh, cigar smoke curling around him. I poked him in the ribs, and he burst into laughter, the sound taking me back to the days when home felt like the safest place in the world.

Joe had some savings, and it wasn't long before he brought up the idea of buying a place. Living with my parents didn't sit right with him, a man who'd been on his own since eighteen.

"I want our own home, love." Taking hold of my hands he spoke full of quiet certainty. "Somewhere we can marry and raise a family. Is that what you want too?"

"Yes, yes, and yes," I grinned, leaping into his arms and pressing my lips against his.

"Thank God for that. For a second, I thought you might be a player." He smirked, teasing.

"Me? A player?" I raised an eyebrow.

"Well, you do have a history with Daniel, the big-shot drug dealer, with you as his trusty sidekick." His eyes twinkled with mischief.

I punched him playfully and we tumbled onto the bed, laughing. We had a plan now, a future laid out in front of us. It felt solid, like nothing could go wrong… but I should have known better than to trust that sentiment.

*****

Moving into the little 'two up, two down' in Solihull felt like settling for less, but it was ours. We needed it to be. Telling Mum and Dad that we wanted to handle it alone, without their help, felt like an act of rebellion. They'd always been there to pick up the pieces in the past, always too involved in the wreckage of my previous relationships. But Joe and I were determined to make it on our own.

Mum waved her hands in that familiar, frantic way, confusion written all over her face. "But with our help, you could have a nice place in Lapworth, near us, couldn't she, Patrick?"

"We're doing this ourselves." I kept my voice firm but calm. I looked to Dad. "You get it, don't you?"

His smile creased at the corners.

"Of course we do. Remember our first home, Nancy? It wasn't much, but it was ours. Let them have this."

Mum's persistence wavered. "Alright, but let me help with the decorating, at least?"

Joe and I couldn't fight her on that. We exchanged a glance and nodded together,

"Yes, Mum. That would be great."

The paperwork for the mortgage consumed us. Joe's laptop had become our lifeline, but an ink spot of darkness was seeping into our life of light and love. One afternoon, while filling out a form, an email popped up. The address was unfamiliar, I clicked it without thinking. My breath hitched. There, staring back at me was something I wished I could unsee. Attached were photos—disturbing, wrong. The message asked to meet Joe again. For a moment the room spun, thoughts swirling in confusion inside me like leaves in a hurricane.

That evening, as soon as Joe stepped through the door, I pounced. "I saw something on your laptop today. An email... from a kid in Manchester. There were naked photos. He wants to meet again. What the hell is going on?"

His face flushed, and his eyes darkened. "No idea. My laptop's been playing up since I left The Hedgeway. I've been getting weird stuff—maybe three emails a week. I just delete them."

I tried to swallow the lump in my throat, but it wouldn't go down. He rolled his eyes and crossed his arms, and I forced a smile, a laugh that felt too forced. "Of course, that makes sense. I knew it had to be something simple." But a chill crept into my bones, one I couldn't shake. *I want to trust you, but do I really know you?*

"I'll get it looked at, I promise. I've just been pushing it aside." He rubbed his arms as if the air had grown cold.

I stepped closer, wrapping him in a hug. "We'll figure it out."

He gave me a smile, but it didn't reach his eyes. I saw something there—something he was holding back. The thought gnawed at me. *Could he have secrets? A child maybe? But why those photos?*

*****

The house slowly became ours, though it felt more like organised chaos. Books stacked high in every corner; dishes abandoned on the kitchen counter. It was a mess, but for once, I didn't care. Joe was thriving at work, and Dad had promoted me to Head of Accounts. I was leading presentations, pitching to new customers and meeting with the bank to arrange a better deal on our long-term loans. It was more than I'd ever imagined.

Cravings came and went in waves, that 'need' that wrecked my life, and never stronger than just before big presentations. My heart would race, palms clammy, the way they used to be before I took coke.

Back then, I thought 'using' made me cool, helped me fit in. I'd stopped during those awkward teenage years, but university had dragged me back in. Jordan and I had tried quitting together, but it did nothing for his temper or my awkwardness. And then there was Daniel—coke had been our thrill, our escape. Selling it became a way to belong, to keep control. As much as I hated to admit it, coke had been an integral part of my life.

Dad caught my eye during a recent presentation. "I trust you." His words wrapped around me like a warm blanket, steadying me. I remembered the downward spiral—coke dragging me to a place I only just escaped from. I was lucky, unlike Daniel. He'd disappeared without a trace, but the memory of him lingered, like a heavy stone around my neck, a reminder of my guilt and greed.

Despite everything, Joe and I were happy—genuinely happy. For the first time in my life, I was content, knowing the future held nothing but blue skies. Dreams of marriage and children became more possible with each passing day. Maybe, after everything, I could finally be the woman I was meant to be—flawed, but honest, and at peace with the path I'd chosen.

Yet, somewhere deep inside, I couldn't shake the feeling that the past wasn't done with me. Not yet.

*****

It was Mum's idea. She had a knack for finding bargains. "I've found a great deal on 'Late Escapes,' two weeks in Puerto De Pollensa at the Hotel Daina. What do you think?"

I almost knocked over my coffee. The idea of sun and sea felt like an impossible dream. "That sounds incredible. We really do need a break." The jolt of joy fell away when I remembered the balance in our bank. "But we're skint. I'm sorry we can't go, Mum. Joe's too proud. He wants us to stand on our own two feet."

She sighed, knowing exactly what I meant. "Joe's always been stubborn when it comes to money. But surely, there's a way to make him see sense."

I shook my head. "I can't think of one."

"We'll pay." That familiar determination filled her voice. "It's our treat. I had a win on the Premium Bonds, and your dad said, 'nothing's too good for our baby girl.'"

I glanced at my phone, checking Joe's schedule. "I know he's due some time off." I couldn't contain my excitement, bouncing around the room, ponytail flying. "Are you sure, Mum? That's a lot of money!"

She smiled, her eyes crinkling. "Come and sit down, you're making me dizzy."

I collapsed onto the sofa, pulling her into a tight hug. "You're the best. Let me talk to Joe. I'll tell him it's a bonus from work. What do you think?"

She squeezed my hand. "Whatever works for you. That's all that matters."

*****

It was our first family holiday, flying out from Manchester for a brilliant deal at a stunning hotel right in the heart of Puerto De Pollensa. Joe had managed to get the time off work, though he needed to stay contactable two days a week. On those days, Mum, Dad, and I planned to explore Mallorca, ticking off Palma and Pollensa markets from our list.

The harbour stretched out before us, a mix of yachts and ships glistening in the evening sun. Most nights, we wandered along the pine walk, the warmth of the setting sun kissing our skin as we soaked in the beauty around us.

There was a little bar tucked in the boatyard that we couldn't stay away from. The owner, a local girl with long dark hair and sharp blue eyes, ruled the place. She didn't take any nonsense from tourists, and everyone knew it. The seating sprawled outside, with steep steps leading down to the water's edge, where the sea stretched out in front of us. It felt magical, like the waves were conjuring their own stories. But I knew the water was treacherous. Deep, dangerous—a beauty with teeth.

From our spot, I could see the hotel where they filmed The Night Manager, nestled in the mountains beyond the super yachts, catamarans, and fishing boats. My eyes always drifted to the traditional wooden sailing boats, their long teak frames cutting through the water with grace. As they set sail, the breeze carried their majesty, the sails catching the wind like dancers twirling towards the horizon.

The salt tingled on my lips, the wind swaying my hips, and for a split second, I could almost imagine being one of those lovers disappearing out to sea. But when a storm rolled in, the harbour turned desolate. The story of Maria and her lover, Tirso, filled the air, whispered between locals making the sign of the cross. I longed to know the tale, but the superstitions kept them tight-lipped.

Mum and Dad headed back to the Daina most evenings for a nightcap, leaving me and Joe to explore the town square. Cheap cocktails and pints of beer flowed at Bony's as we people-watched and laughed. The square came alive with street performers—guitarists, balloon artists, flame throwers, acrobats—each lighting up the night as they drifted past looking for tips.

It was easy to imagine my old self here, making friends, selling coke, and raking in cash. But that life felt far away now. I watched Joe, admiring his build, his chiselled face. No wonder he was so vain.

I started singing, half teasing. "You walked into the party like you were walking onto a ship."

Joe grinned, took a long swig of beer, and joined in, "You're so vain, I bet you think this song is about us."

I leaned in, "Don't you, don't you?"

He laughed, pulling me close. "Alright, Carly Simon, you've made your point. Let's have one last drink at the Lemon Tree."

To a round of applause, we bowed, then linked arms and strolled down towards the market stalls, passing the beach until we found our spot. The Lemon Tree was one of our favourites. We sat with a view that swept across the harbour, watching the world pass by. Aperol spritzes, olives, and Manchego cheese arrived at our table, and we clinked our glasses.

With his eyes far away taking in the boats, Joe sighed. "This is the life. I can't believe we're heading back tomorrow."

I rested my head in my hands. "Back to work, back to the cold. This trip's been amazing."

Joe stretched, yawning. "It's not all bad. Come on, early start tomorrow."

Rubbing my tired eyes, I smiled. "I've loved the sun... and being with you. But yeah, I'm wiped out."

Hand in hand, we wandered back to the hotel, neither of us knowing what awaited us the next day.

Chapter 14

Joe—Lucy v Becky

THE FIRST TIME I laid eyes on Lucy at The Hedgeway, I pegged her as another trust-fund kid dragged into rehab to save her allowance. She looked the part—bleached hair with two inches of brown roots, piercing blue eyes, a voice that had been fine-tuned by the company she'd kept. But there was something else too. Something that caught my attention, though I knew I shouldn't have been intrigued.

At first, I told myself it was nothing. Just curiosity. But the more I got to know her story, the more I understood her. Her past relationships, the men she'd been with, it all made sense—why she desperately craved attention, why she played up her vulnerability like it was her only currency. But once I saw the why behind it all, it wasn't just curiosity anymore.

But I was living with Becky and should have kept my wandering thoughts under control. We were coasting along in a way that felt comfortable but never quite right. There had always been this hard edge to her, something I ignored for the sake of peace.

When I asked what she thought of Lucy after one of the earlier sessions, her response had been so cold, it caught me off guard. She'd waved a dismissive hand. "She's trouble. A rich, spoiled no-hoper, that one. I knew her in Lapworth, back when she was messing around with Jeff. Some people never change."

Stepping back with my heart beating fast, "That's kind of mean of you!"

"Look, we've got history and the thing that bugs me is that she doesn't even remember! Her mum and mine were friends back in the day, but that didn't last once she met her rich man."

"Oh, I didn't know that."

"Mum and I would look after Lucy whilst her mum went out on dates. Our paths crossed again for a while at school and then in again in Lapworth's disused station some years later, but nothing after I went to London and reinvented myself."

"Why haven't you said hello?"

"We had a brief chat on her second day but she doesn't really remember me. Only the time when I was in my hippy phase. I am going to observe her from the sidelines and bide my time."

"What do you mean?"

A mean glint sparkled in her eyes. "Revenge is a dish best served cold."

"I've never seen this side of you before." It was then I knew I had to tread carefully.

As a true Scorpio, I've always rushed in like a knight in shining armour, ready to rescue damsels in distress. I know that about myself, and Becky's onerous life has always tugged at my heartstrings, sparking my urge to protect her. After her mother's overdose, the care workers reached out to her father, but he wanted nothing to do with her. He claimed he had recently married and that Hazel was just a one-night stand. Becky later tried reconnecting in her teens, but he, ever the cold-hearted swine, wished her well and rejected her again.

Our recent conversation stuck with me, more for the venom she released than the words she spoke. That was when I began to see Becky for what she really was, her slipped mask revealing something harder, colder.

I found myself thinking about Lucy more than I should have, and before long, I moved her out of my sessions and into Becky's, hoping that some distance would help. It didn't. She was still there, in the back of my mind, every time I closed my eyes.

The day we climbed the wall, when I saw her laughing, free in a way I hadn't seen before—it hit me like a truck. There was something deeper there, something that shook me. And for the first time, I couldn't ignore it.

I'd never felt anything like it before. It was more than just attraction, more than the fleeting rushes I'd experienced in the past. This was deeper.

In that moment, I realized what had been missing in every relationship I'd ever had. The connection with Lucy wasn't just physical; it was emotional, something that settled in my chest and made my heart pound. The way she looked at me, like she could see the real me, scared and excited me at the same time. It was terrifying to feel so vulnerable, but there was warmth that came with it, like I was finally home.

Then sitting opposite her in the café something clicked. The more I thought about her, the clearer it became—nothing I'd experienced before came close to this. The casual flings, the half-hearted relationships, even Becky who I thought I had loved—they paled in comparison to this.

This was all-consuming, like my world had narrowed to just her. Everything else dulled, like background noise. The way she made me laugh, the way her presence settled me—it was like she filled gaps I never knew existed.

I had finally found the love of my life, and for the first time, I understood what it meant to be truly in love. It was terrifying, exhilarating, and utterly undeniable.

As soon as we returned to The Hedgeway, I was summoned into my manager's office where I was told in no uncertain terms that I was no longer required. I had breached their trust and failed to turn up for a couple of meetings that afternoon.

I knew Becky would have sold me down the river, but I hadn't expected her to throw all my clothes out of the window. When I got to our room, she folded her arms and glared at me.

"Come on Becky, let's be grown up about this."

"Get lost and get out. I never want to speak to you again. Take that tart with you—you're both losers!"

"Becky, I never meant for this to happen. I did love you and want us to part as friends."

With tears streaming down her face, I saw her jaw clench. "I have something I'll keep for you. It may one day change your life for the better!"

"What do you mean… may change my life? Becky, tell me!"

Tapping her nose, "A surprise is better, I think. I hope you like it."

I recoiled, wondering what on earth she planned to do.

"Now get the hell out of *my* room before I get back from the counselling session with your *druggy girlfriend!*"

Thankfully, she hadn't thrown my laptop out of the window. I shoved it under my arm, grabbed bin bags and ran outside to pick up my clothes as fast as I could. I needed to get to Lucy as quickly as possible.

Reaching Lucy's room, I knocked, praying to God that it wasn't all just a dream.

"Come in."

For the first time in my life, I had butterflies. *Was the moment in the café real?*

"I thought you would come straight here." She's stood by the window, still in that damn sexy mini skirt and a flimsy blouse, yet even with red lipstick, she looked innocent and vulnerable.

I took her in my arms and discovered the true meaning of 'coming home' and being where I belonged. I sniffed her musky, floral scented hair. "I want you."

With eyes sparkling, "Yes, I can tell!"

"But you have to go to your last session with Becky after dinner."

Biting her lip, Lucy sat on the bed, her shoulders tense. "I thought about skipping it altogether, but I can't keep avoiding things. I need to face her, apologise; see if she'll accept it. But I really don't want to go." Her voice wavered, and the conflict in her eyes said it all.

"They won't let you leave unless you do," I reminded her. "You signed the Terms and Conditions when you got here. You have to see it through. I'll be waiting when you're done." I pressed soft kisses to her neck and she melted against me. I wished I could help her face Becky. My arms tightened around her fragile body.

It took everything in me to let her go, to watch her walk out, knowing this had to be done on her own. Once she was gone though, pacing the floor became my only option. Becky's face kept flashing in my mind—how cold she'd looked when she talked about Lucy. Something about it stuck with me, gnawed at me.

Trying to read while I waited didn't ease my growing nerves as I watched the minutes tick by. When the time for her appointment came I knew needed to be close and make sure she was okay. Before I knew it, I was rushing down the hallway towards Becky's office, my heart thumping.

The minutes dragged as I paced the corridor, each one heavier than the last. Becky could be ruthless, and I knew she wouldn't hold back. The idea of her tearing Lucy down made me want to barge in, but I needed a clean exit from this place, and I couldn't risk making things worse. I clenched my fists, waiting, helpless.

Finally, Lucy emerged, stress written all over her face. The moment we embraced, a gut-wrenching scream echoed through the hall—a sound so raw and feral it made my blood run cold.

We froze as Ben, one of the other counsellors, sprinted past us and threw open the door to Becky's office. She was curled up in the corner, trembling, her eyes wild, scowling at the walls like she was seeing something none of us could.

Ben knelt beside her, pulling her into his arms, murmuring something I couldn't hear as she whimpered and slowly quieted. His face flushed with anger when he glanced up at me. "Shut the bloody door. This isn't a show for you to watch. Go away, you've done enough. Now!"

I clenched my jaw, forcing myself to stay calm as I closed the door. Lucy squeezed my hand, but the burden of responsibility knocked me for six. This was my fault and I didn't know how to fix it.

*****

The next morning, as I turned to say goodbye to The Hedgeway, a wave of guilt crashed over me. Contrition clung to my skin like a bad smell, a reminder of what I had done to Becky, making me feel repulsive. I couldn't shake the thought of her parting words: "I've kept a present for you, something that may change your life for the better." Her voice echoed in my head, filling me with dread. *What did she mean by that?*

Patrick and Nancy welcomed me into their home with open arms from the start, treating me like family. Nothing felt off-limits with them. They helped me find a job, and today, I am happier than I ever thought possible. I have the love of my life, a great family, a good job, and friends. More importantly, I'd managed to keep my self-respect through it all.

*****

Five months later, Lucy and I had bought our first home together, securing a mortgage despite her parents' insistence on helping. I knew it was the right thing to do—to stand on our own two feet, even if it disappointed them. Everything had fallen into place.

But there was one shadow looming over this perfect picture—the constant stream of texts and emails that kept popping up. Every time my phone buzzed, I swear I lost a year off my lifespan. I couldn't bring myself to tell Lucy why I was getting these messages. She would lose it if she knew about them.

It wasn't just the fear of her finding out. I worried about what it might do to her—how fragile she still seemed at times. After everything she'd been through—rehab, battling her past, those moments of crippling self-doubt—I couldn't risk pushing her over the edge.

I had seen what it looked like when she slipped, when the horror of everything sent her spiralling into that dark place where old scars still lingered. The thought of her falling back into those patterns of self-harm or depression haunted me. Even now, knowing how much she'd fought to reclaim herself, I couldn't shake the fear.

I needed to protect her—not just from the world outside, but from the dark corners of her own mind, the parts that this brewing trouble with Becky might stir up. She had already started to shed the layers that once defined her, letting her bleached blonde hair grow out and declaring she wanted her 'normal' back.

It wasn't just her appearance; it was her way of reclaiming control, bit by bit. Her natural chestnut brown hair framed her sky-blue eyes, making them brighter, clearer. But I couldn't help wondering if this change was more than just skin deep. Was she truly finding herself again, or hiding behind a new mask—one I couldn't see through?

The other day, she had been using my laptop when a suspicious email came through. I still remembered how the conversation unfolded later that evening.

"Sweetheart, I was on your laptop, and this email came through with a weird title and attachments. I didn't open it, just deleted it. Is that okay? What's going on?"

I had brushed it off, offering some half-baked excuse about needing to get the laptop checked. But I hadn't done anything about it.

When her birthday came around two weeks later, I seized the opportunity and bought her a new laptop as a gift, thinking that would solve the problem. I breathed a sigh of relief, but deep down, I knew this wasn't over. I had dodged a bullet, but for how long?

*****

It was hard to contain my excitement the day she came home and mentioned the holiday. A break away with Lucy and her parents—it sounded perfect. But reality hit me hard. Could we afford it now, with the mortgage interest rates climbing every month?

A sigh slipped out as I slumped in the chair. "It sounds amazing, but with the new house and the bills... we can't say yes, Lucy. Your parents have already given us so much."

Lucy knelt in front of me, putting a hand on my knee, her face full of excitement. "It's not a free holiday, sweetheart. I completely agree with you about hand-outs. It's from my bonus at work for landing all those new orders."

I raised one eyebrow at her. "But your boss is your dad, bit convenient."

She slapped my knee, and not too softly. "Hey, I'll have you know the business is booming since I started working there again. This has nothing to do with who I am but what I have accomplished."

A flicker of hope surged through me. I grabbed her hand, pulling her close as we broke into a wobbly salsa, laughing. "Well, that changes everything! Of course we'll go. I wouldn't miss it for the world—time away with my favourite people. When are we leaving?"

She beamed, bouncing on her toes. "The week after next, for two whole weeks. Is that alright?"

I nodded, the excitement bubbling up again. "I might have to take my laptop and do a bit of work from Puerto de Pollensa for a few days, but I can shift clients around. It'll be fine. How about we go out tonight, celebrate our good fortune? The Tablet in Dorridge sounds perfect."

Her smile widened. "It's exactly what we need."

*****

The holiday arrived faster than I expected, and soon enough, we touched down in Palma. Patrick and I exchanged a quick glance as we headed to the rental desk, the unspoken bond of being the designated drivers. The roads felt strange at first, the car hugging the wrong side, but after a few nervous turns, we settled into the rhythm.

Lucy sat behind us, her voice full of excitement as she pointed out the giant red wine bottle and the oversized snail signs along the motorway, trying to pull travellers toward the next junction.

Half listening to her, I chuckled, but my mind was elsewhere—on the jagged peaks of the Tramontana Mountains looming ahead. Those mountains reached out to me, and I couldn't wait to tackle them in the coming days with Lucy at my side.

As we pulled into the Daina car park, the air felt different—lighter, crisper. The location was a dream. Mountains framed the landscape behind us, and everywhere I looked, the sea stretched out, impossibly blue. White sails dotted the horizon, speedboats zipped by, and parasailers floated above the water like colourful birds. Even the fishing vessels sprang to life and became part of a grander picture, bobbing in time with the rhythm of the island.

The streets buzzed with life. Hotels no taller than six stories lined the coast, nestled between bars and cafés. Cyclists, all Lycra-clad, lounged under a tangle of umbrellas, sipping coffee and chatting as the sun bathed them in warmth. The scent of salt hung in the air, mingling with the rich aroma of roasting fish from nearby beachside grills.

"Look at this place, Lucy." My eyes soaked it all in. "It's got everything—the vibe, the character. It still feels like Mallorca, not some tourist trap."

Lucy nodded, her eyes gleaming with the same wonder. "It's beautiful. There's so much to explore—so many walks, trails, and all the fresh fish. I could live off it."

A wide grin spread across my face. "If we could stay here, right by the sea, I'd never want to leave." The breeze ruffled my hair as I glanced out to the horizon.

She wrapped her arms around my waist, pulling me close. "One day, maybe we'll have a place here of our own."

I grinned down at her, lifting a hand to trace a finger across her cheek. "By the way I don't know if I have ever told you, but I love your freckles." I leaned down and kissed her freckly nose. She giggled and buried her head in my jumper.

The days slipped by in a sun-drenched blur. We wandered together, our laughter filling the quiet streets, our conversations easy. Life felt perfect, almost unnervingly so.

Patrick put his back out giving me a rowing race, but other than that every day was heaven on Earth.

On the day we left, I paused for one last look at the sea. I tipped my head back, breathing in the cool air, trying to imprint every detail on my memory. *Maybe next year,* I thought, as the waves lapped the shore in their eternal dance.

Chapter 15

Joe—Caught in the Web

LANDING IN MANCHESTER late at night wasn't ideal, especially with the long journey back to Solihull still ahead of us. To make things easier, Patrick had pre-paid a Solihull taxi company to pick us up and drive us home.

The baggage claim was nearly empty, just a handful of people from our flight waiting in silence for their luggage. An uneasy stillness hung in the air, broken only by the occasional shuffle of feet. The sight of several police officers and airport staff milling around the quiet area felt strange and quite unsettling.

Lucy tapped her fingers restlessly on the seat beside her, her gaze darting to the clock on the wall. "Who takes a child on a flight at this time of night?" Every inch of her oozed frustration.

I leaned back in my seat with a sigh. "Overnight flights are cheaper. We'll probably do the same one day, so give them a break."

She managed a faint smile, but her shoulders sagged. "Sorry, I didn't think." She dropped her head into her hands, exhaustion catching up with her.

Nancy, oblivious to the earlier exchange, suddenly spoke up. "Come on, Darling, the children are tired and want to sleep. Lift your head and calm down."

Lucy shuffled closer to me with a sigh. I put an arm around her. "I've had a great holiday. Thanks for making it happen with that bonus. Hopefully, there'll be another one next year."

Across from us, Patrick shot Nancy a questioning look. She gave him a tight-lipped smile and patted his hand. "I'll explain later."

The conveyor belt whirred into life, and everyone jumped up, crowding around it. I stayed back, content to wait, but Lucy nudged me, her eyes lighting up. "I think I see our leopard print cases—there, just coming out. What luck."

I stood, making my way over purposefully. The cases rolled towards me, the only ones to emerge so far. I grabbed them and turned back towards Lucy, throwing her a grin as I high-fived her. But before I could take another step, a police officer blocked my path.

A firm hand rested on the handle of one suitcase. "Sir, could you show me your passport?"

"Sure." With nausea rising and a shaking hand, I handed it over. "Is there something wrong?" A weird sensation of guilt washed over me, even though I hadn't done anything wrong. He kept hold of my passport I noted with rising stress levels.

"Are these your suitcases, sir?" His measured tone matched the sharpness in his eyes.

I nodded, my heart skipping a beat.

The officer motioned for me to follow; his expression unreadable. I glanced back at Lucy, placing my hand over my face in disbelief. She furrowed her brow, gesturing that she'd catch up once she had her parents' bags.

In an impersonal room off the baggage reclaim area, another officer stood waiting. The suitcases were both put on the table. "Can you open them, sir?"

I unzipped the first case, my heart thudding in my chest as they rummaged through it. They pulled out my laptop, and another officer stepped forward. "Can you hand over your phone, sir? After you've unlocked it."

I frowned. "Is that necessary? We've just had a long flight—we just want to get home."

"I understand, sir, but we're following up on a tip-off. We'll be as quick as possible."

"A tip-off? From who?"

"I'm afraid I can't disclose that," the officer replied, his tone flat.

Two of the officers moved to a nearby table, leaving one with me, silent and watchful. The wait dragged on, each second tightening the knot in my stomach. When they finally returned, one of them stepped forward.

"Joseph Browne, I am arresting you on suspicion of possessing child pornography on your laptop and phone. You have the right to remain silent…"

The words hit like a punch to the gut. My head spun, and all I could manage was, "You've got the wrong person."

Before I could process what was happening, Lucy appeared in the doorway, her parents hanging back as she confronted the officers. "Why are you stopping Joe? Why are you going through our bags?"

One of the officers shifted his stance, glancing at the suitcases. "Miss, can you confirm which of these cases is yours?"

Lucy's face flushed red with frustration. "My clothes are in both cases. Can I talk to Joe?"

One of the officers glanced at me. "Do you want to speak to her?"

I threw my arms up. "Of course, I do."

"You've got two minutes," the officer said. "Then we'll have to take him to the station."

Lucy's eyes narrowed, panic creeping into her voice. "What the hell is going on? Why are they taking you?"

I tried to calm her, but the words felt hollow. "It's a mistake, love. They think they've found something on my laptop and phone."

Her face twisted in confusion. "What did they find?"

I rubbed my hands on my trousers, struggling to find the right words. "They're saying child pornography. I don't know how it got there I swear."

Before she could respond, the officer interrupted. "Sorry, but we have to go now."

Tears welled up in Lucy's eyes as I reached out, but a policeman stepped between us, cutting off any comfort I could offer. I forced a smile, though it felt unnatural. "Don't worry. I'll see you at home. It's all a mistake."

They cuffed me, and as they led me away, Lucy's voice cut through the chatter of onlookers. "The show's over, people! Go home!"

I glanced back to see Nancy and Patrick catching her as she collapsed into their arms. Their eyes met mine, cold and full of disdain, I was already guilty in their minds.

*****

The cold air in the holding cell pressed against my skin, making the already suffocating atmosphere heavy. My thoughts spun wildly, but my body remained frozen, unresponsive. They'd taken everything—belt, watch, phone—and left me in my own clothes, a strange attempt to preserve my dignity while stripping me of everything else.

When the officer returned, I struggled to register what he was saying. "Five minutes, then you can make your call."

The fluorescent lights above buzzed as I followed him down a narrow corridor. It felt like I was walking towards a fate that had already been sealed. The holding area phone loomed ahead, the single lifeline in this nightmare.

I dialled the number of someone I knew from my school days who I followed on LinkedIn. The man had become a prestigious lawyer and I'd always been rather proud of knowing him. Still, I'd not spoken to him in years and my fingers trembled as I pressed each digit. I sent a silent prayer up that he would answer at this time in the morning.

"William Locke here."

"It's Joe Browne," I said, my voice catching. "We were at boarding school together. You knew me as Joey Browne."

There was a brief pause on the line. "Of course, I remember you. What's going on?"

"I'm in trouble, William. Arrested. They're saying I've got child pornography on my laptop and phone. It's not true. I swear it. They've put me in a holding cell in Wythenshawe Police Station. You're my one call."

I heard him sigh deeply before responding. "Alright, I'm coming down. It will take me a few hours to get there. Don't say a word until I'm with you, Joe. Not a word."

The line went dead, and the seriousness of my situation bore down on me. The officer led me back to the cell, where a cold cup of tea and a wrapped cheese sandwich sat waiting on a plastic tray. I pushed it aside, my appetite lost to the fear nibbling at my insides. My mind flashed back to Lucy's face when they had cuffed me. *God, what have I dragged her into?*

Nearly three hours later, as promised, William arrived. He was a familiar figure in an unfamiliar place, a brief beacon of hope as they led me to an interview room. I wasn't sure what to expect, but seeing him, as sharp as ever, gave me the first hint of relief.

"Joe." He shook my hand firmly. "Let's skip the pleasantries and get to work. We've got an hour. Tell me everything, from the start."

"Sorry to call you in the middle of the night."

He waved it off. "Happens all the time. Now tell me everything you know."

I gave him the rundown—our flight back from Palma, the police stopping me as soon as I grabbed the bags, the anonymous tip-off that turned my life upside down. As I spoke, a dark thought surfaced, a memory I'd tried to bury.

"When I left my ex, Becky, she told me I'd have a 'surprise' that would change my life. She can be vindictive. I didn't take it seriously at the time."

William's eyes narrowed. "Did Becky have access to your laptop? Your phone?"

I nodded. "Yes, we shared everything. Passwords, devices. It ended badly when I left her for someone else."

"And when did the emails and texts start?"

"Right around the breakup," I said, the pieces finally clicking into place. "I ignored them, filed them away on my laptop, kept the texts but never responded. Stupid, I know."

William gave me a long look, his mouth a thin line. "Naive, but not surprising."

I shifted uncomfortably. "My wife found one of the emails. I told her I'd deal with it, but… I never did."

"And you never replied to any of them?"

"No," I shook my head. "I thought if I ignored it, it would stop."

William's lips curled into a humourless smile. "Still burying your head in the sand, eh, Joe? What's this ex's full name?"

"Becky Locke." A wave of nausea swept over me as I said her name aloud. "Do you think she could've done this?"

William's eyes darkened. "I'd bet my career on it. You've got to be careful with scorned women with grudges. I'll look into it. Is she still at The Hedgeway do you know?"

I shook my head. "I don't, but here's what I know." I told him everything I knew about her, the worry of it all starting to crush me. William scribbled furiously; his jaw clenched. "She's had some bad breaks in life, but that doesn't excuse this. I'll make a few calls. We've got twenty minutes before the interview starts."

My mouth went dry, and I struggled to find my voice. "Do you think we have a chance?"

William's confidence was unwavering. "Absolutely. Trust me, Joe. Just follow my lead in there, and we'll get through this."

Back in the cell, I slumped onto the bed, exhaustion pulling at me. But one thought kept spinning in my mind—Becky's last words. That she'd give me a surprise that would change my life. It was coming back to haunt me; a cruel game I hadn't realised I was playing. And now, it was too late to turn back. At sunrise, with the sound of early morning traffic drifting through the walls, I paced the cell, something niggled away at me. Something I should have noticed but couldn't quite grasp.

*****

The interview room felt like a cage, small and airless, with four chairs and a recording device that seemed to pulse with anticipation. Two officers sat across from me, their expressions neutral but their eyes sharp, like they'd already decided my fate. William sat beside me, his presence a lifeline, though my nerves were fraying by the second.

The lead officer introduced himself and the other officer, his tone clipped and formal. He rattled off the purpose of the interview, explaining the child pornography offence they were investigating, making sure I knew the interview was being recorded. His words washed over me in waves—procedural, detached—yet every sentence hit like a hammer. My heart pounded as he reminded me that I didn't have to say anything, but whatever I did say could be used against me in court.

My legs felt weak beneath the table, the air thick with dread.

William placed a firm hand on my arm as the officer cautioned me, grounding me as the room spun. "Would you like some water, Joe?"

I shook my head. "No. Let's just get this over with."

The questioning began. The officers fired off a barrage of questions—my whereabouts on specific dates, whether I knew the people sending me the messages, asking for details I had no idea about. I could feel their gaze burning into me, waiting for any slip, any crack in my defence.

But I stayed silent, uttering the words William had coached me on: "No comment."

William took over, calmly weaving through the mess I'd found myself in. He brought up Becky, the threats she'd made, the timing of it all. He painted the picture of someone spiteful, vengeful, trying to ruin me after our messy breakup. As he spoke, I could see the officers' faces flicker with interest, but nothing more. They weren't buying it, not yet.

Finally, the interview ended, and they escorted me back to my cell. The claustrophobia hit again, but William gave me a glimmer of hope. He promised to investigate, to get to the bottom of everything, and left with Lucy's number to keep her updated.

The next day, William returned. His expression was tight, and something in his eyes filled me with despondency—something had changed, I could see it in his eyes. He dropped a plastic bag onto the table between us. Inside was a burner phone. My heart stopped.

"Let me tell you what I learned from Becky," William said, folding his arms, his voice sharp. "She admitted she made that 'surprise' comment when you split, and she used your laptop for work. She showed me her new laptop, claimed she'd moved her files there the day you left. Then, she went to a chest of drawers and pulled out this."

He nodded at the phone, still encased in the bag like it was evidence from a crime scene—which, of course, it was.

"She told me this is your other phone."

I stared at it, my mouth dry, bile rising in my throat.

"I put on gloves, transferred the phone into this bag, then asked her for the charger. We plugged it in, and once it powered up, I saw a string of messages, stopping about nine months ago. The content was… disturbing. They suggested you were meeting children on your days off."

I couldn't breathe. My vision swam. "She—she's lying. You know she is. You believe me, don't you?"

William didn't answer right away. His face was set, conflicted.

"I checked your rota, Joe. The dates match."

A cold chill ran down my spine. I gripped the table to steady myself. "This is Becky's doing. It's her phone, William. You have to believe me."

His expression softened slightly, but then he dropped the next bombshell. "We ran prints on the phone. There are two sets, Joe. Yours and Becky's."

The ground disappeared beneath me. With the room spinning, I sank my head into my hands, everything crushing down on me. Every word felt like a nail in my coffin.

After what felt like an eternity, I lifted my head, teeth gritted. "So what now?"

William exhaled slowly, his voice low. "We'll have to hand the phone over to the police. Let them run their checks. If we don't have any other way out… I suggest considering a plea deal. It's not what you want to hear, but unless you can prove your innocence, it may be the best option."

A plea deal. The words echoed in my head, like a death sentence.

“I need time,” I said quietly, my voice hollow. “Time to think.”

William nodded, rising from his seat. “I’ll tell Lucy. She needs to know.”

As he walked out of the room, I began to sink, drowning in a nightmare with no end in sight. And the worst part? I wasn’t sure I’d ever wake up from it.

Chapter 16

Patrick—Bad Karma

MY BABY GIRL was slipping away, piece by piece. The light in her eyes had dulled, swallowed by the familiar darkness she refused to speak about. She wouldn't mention Joe, but bulimia had returned, dragging her into its suffocating embrace. She kept her focus on work, trying to carry on, but her spark had vanished. It tore at me. Nancy, too, had lost her mind over it, muttering over and over about being cursed.

I'd always faced problems head-on, never one to back down. But now, I found myself stuck. Trapped in this situation, my hands tied as Lucy spiralled. I'd hear her phone buzz, the soft click as she ended the call, a tear gathering in her eye every time. It had to be Joe. Of course it was. We'd told her to stay away, but she couldn't let go. Evidence of his guilt had piled up, a mountain of proof, but I knew Lucy didn't want to believe it.

I thought back to the men who had passed through her life, the ones I'd tried to shield her from. Each one leaving a scar, and me trying every time to patch her up. Lucy and Nancy were my world. I didn't have anyone else, not since my own family turned their backs on me when I married Nancy. My love for them was enough though. Or so I'd always told myself.

All those years ago, when I took the contract to renovate the mother and baby shelter, I never imagined how it would shift everything. I hadn't expected to see Hazel there—Hazel, the one-night stand I wished I could erase. She'd been babysitting Lucy with her daughter, Becky. It had hit me like a gut punch. Could Becky be mine? Nancy trusted me, believed in me, and I clung to that. I owed Hazel something, though. For not spilling the truth.

My mind wandered back to that conversation, two years before our paths crossed again at the shelter. Hazel's words still echoed in my ears. "I'm pregnant, and you're the father. So, what are you going to do about it?" Her accusation had hung between us, heavy and damning.

I'd been blunt, maybe too cold. "I can't help you. It was a one-night stand. I don't know if the baby's mine. I'll pay for an abortion, but I need proof of the appointment. You're using drugs, Hazel. Bringing a baby into that mess isn't right."

Her reply had been a curse, spat out with venom. "Patrick Platt—you're a bastard and a half."

Maybe a truer word had never been spoken, but I needed to make sure she didn't bad-mouth me to Nancy so I placated her with a roll of money and a bag of the white stuff.

I'd assumed Hazel had ended the pregnancy. I'd hoped, anyway. A child born into her world of booze and drugs, what kind of life would that be? When I saw her again, Becky by her side, it all came rushing back. I tried to dig around for details, to figure out if Becky could be mine, but I never found an answer. Eventually, I buried the thought, focusing on my life with Nancy and Lucy.

When Hazel overdosed, I'd received a call. Her social worker told me Hazel had put my name on Becky's birth certificate. They asked if I wanted to take her in, or give her up for adoption. I requested a DNA test, but the social worker wasn't interested. "Let's stick with the adoption if you're not sure," she'd said. It was a relief. I didn't have to explain anything to Nancy, didn't have to confront a truth I wasn't ready to face.

When the call came from the shelter to inform Nancy of her death, I wrote the details on a note and 'forgot' to pass it over for a week. Nancy struggled enough without adding a funeral to her list of things to cope with. Besides, I couldn't take the risk that someone might mention that Becky might be mine. That would be a disaster too many for my wife.

Years passed. Our paths still crossed now and then. To my horror, Becky ended up at Lucy's school, pulling Alice, Lucy's best friend, away, though she was two years older. I wouldn't say it was intentional, but it showed the kind of person Becky had become. I'd dodged a bullet, and I thanked whatever fate had kept her out of my life. In hindsight it was obvious that all of Lucy's problems began the day Becky arrived at her school.

But Jeff tangled everything up. When I saw him with Becky at the derelict railway station, my blood ran cold. That boy was a parasite, no good for anyone—especially not Lucy. Even so, I wasn't about to let Becky take Lucy's boyfriend away from her, just like she'd taken Alice. So, I made sure Jeff disappeared. I figured it was better for Lucy to not know where he'd gone than to have him leave her for Becky. A pair of concrete shoes and Earlswood Lakes took care of the rest.

Lucy had been suspicious, asking too many questions about Jeff's disappearance. I could see her mind working, piecing things together, but the chances of anyone finding him were slim. Unless they dredged the lakes—and that wouldn't happen in our lifetime. Becky took off to London, and I'd felt nothing but relief.

My daughter remained broken for months. It hurt to watch, but somehow, she pulled herself back. Finding her way to university and then to Jordan. He'd been perfect—too good to be true. Full of charm, successful, and riding high on Lucy's love for him. Posh house, fancy dinners, a woman who adored him—what more did a man need? But Jordan always needed more, vile and unacceptable things.

By the time he was done with Lucy, she was a shadow of herself. What he put her through—years of mental abuse, locking her in that wardrobe, torturing her emotionally—will never leave me. Yet, Lucy's fight, her spirit, that gave me a sliver of pride. When she'd confronted him at his office, the way she stood her ground, I'd never been prouder. The joy in Nancy's voice when she told me about it still echoes.

Jordan had the nerve to call me afterwards. He wanted his share of the house. After everything he'd done to Lucy, he still had the audacity to ask for money. He rambled on about how much the house had increased in value since *he'd* been taking care of it… my blood boiled.

"I'll meet you outside the house next Tuesday, Jordan, ten o'clock. We can discuss what's fair."

"That's a bit late isn't it?"

"I'm working all day; it's then or not at all."

His smug reply grated. "I'll wait for you inside."

I stayed calm. "You won't be able to get in. We've changed the locks. For Lucy's safety, I'm sure you understand."

He spat out, "Well, what a surprise. Baby Girl's precious, isn't she?"

Tuesday rolled around, and sure enough, there he stood. Hands in his pockets, looking like he hadn't a care in the world.

"Evening, Patrick. Hope you've brought my money."

I nodded towards Sid, who stood a few feet away from me. "I'm sure you remember Sid."

Jordan gave him a glance and smirked. "The old Dick detective? Yes, I remember."

"We'll go around the back," I said. "Got something to show you."

He rolled his eyes. "I haven't got long, Patrick. Places to be, you know how it is."

We walked around the house. "Finally doing the patio," I said. "Thought you'd like to see it before the place goes on the market."

Jordan laughed. "That'll bring in some extra cash. I always liked you, Patrick. Too bad Lucy wasn't more like you. We both know why she wasn't, don't we?"

I stepped back, letting his words hang in the air. "She's more like me than you think."

Lucy emerged from behind the bushes, her eyes sharp with fury. "Not such a doormat after all!"

She swung the spade down on his head. Jordan dropped, blood spilling from his scalp as he screamed. "You nasty bit—"

Lucy cut him off with another whack to the head. "Take that, you bastard! If I had my way, I'd bury you alive... see how *you* like being confined to small dark places."

Jordan turned on his side and tried to get up, but Sid and I pinned him down. A cushion over his mouth, we pressed until the fight drained out of him. The concrete was still wet, waiting for him. Together, we dragged his body into the fresh mix.

It took an hour, maybe more, before Sid arrived back from the yard with another load of ready-mix. We poured the rest, smoothing it over until the patio gleamed sparkling new.

Lucy stared at the finished work, her lips curling into a grin. "I think we'll get a good price for the house, even with a sitting tenant. Should've buried a rent book with him!"

I couldn't help but smile at her. Keeping the house in our name had been instinct. "Wait till they get married," I'd said to Nancy when we first offered them the house. At least that had been the right move.

Lucy's nightmares about Jordan didn't stop, though. She knew he was dead, but it didn't matter. Every time she went for a run, I'd stand watch outside, making sure she felt safe. Even then, she'd come back shaken, swearing she'd seen him.

Going to London changed things. It was the making of her. Nancy and I couldn't have been prouder when Lucy got her job and the loft apartment. She reinvented herself, becoming a blonde bombshell, all sleek composure and control. The bulimia stopped and for the first time in years she looked healthy.

Then Daniel showed up. Handsome, well-dressed, dripping in gold, but I had a sixth sense that he had a dark side to him. I spotted it the moment we met. A 'waster' I called him. Too polished, too slick. He played the part well—always kind to the family—but underneath, I could sense it. Something rotten.

One evening, I watched him closely, his smile a little too easy. A quiet pause settled between us. "So, what's your line of work?"

"PE teacher at a local school," he said, flashing that gold tooth of his, the one that matched his chain.

"I hope you don't mind me asking, but how do you and Lucy afford such a nice penthouse?"

Lucy glared at me. "Dad, it's none of your business. Be happy for me."

Nancy nudged me, giving me that look.

But when he showed up at our house recovering from a 'fall' a month later, it all clicked into place. Sid did some digging, and the truth came out. Daniel and Lucy were dealing drugs, stepping on Samuel Sampson's patch. Of all the drug dealers in the world, Samuel Sampson ranked top for brutality.

A street-hardened private eye, Sid had seen everything, rarely getting rattled. But his face told me I should be afraid. "They've got to get out of London, fast," he'd said. Within weeks, they were back under our roof.

Daniel's proposal was the final straw, I had to act. Breaking into his phone was child's play, his pin his birth date. Finding exactly what I needed straight away, I took photos of his contacts and recent messages, and then forwarded them to Sid.

The gang came, as arranged. Sid had been clear about what the deal was and that none of us were to be hurt, but Samuel didn't class Rufus as family. Guns were pointed, and we lost a member of our family. It didn't sit well with me.

Lucy saved us that day. The way she locked Daniel in the walk-in freezer and stormed into the lounge, her bravery will stay with me forever. Owning up to contacting the gang, not knowing if Daniel was alive or dead—that's a weight I will carry to my graves and I don't think either women in my life will ever truly forgive me.

Chapter 17

Lucy—the Final Call

I STARED AT THE phone, the screen lighting up with Joe's name. My hand hovered over the button, and I hesitated, knowing what was coming. Finally, I pressed 'answer.'

"What do you want?" My voice came out sharper than I intended, but I didn't care, I needed to stop loving him.

On the other end, I could hear him pacing. His breath uneven, like a man caged.

"Lucy, please. Don't hang up. I swear, I didn't do it. I promise you—on my life."

My jaw tightened. "The evidence is there, Joe. It's staring us all in the face."

"No. It's wrong." His voice cracked, desperate. "I need your help. I need you, Patrick, and Sid to do some digging. Please. Will you do that for me?"

I shouted, "What is it, Joe? Spit it out. I've got a job to do, bills to pay. You think I've got time for your wild theories?"

"I-I need you to-to find a connection between William and Becky. It's a long shot, but… I'm innocent."

His words hit me like a punch to the gut. My mind swirled, trying to make sense of it. "William Locke? Why did you call him?"

"We went to boarding school together. I mentioned him before, right?"

I closed my eyes, clenching my fists. Memories trickled back, vague and distant. "I think… yeah, I remember you talking about him."

"There's more. The business card he left with me just wouldn't stop bugging me. So, I asked him about his and Becky's surname being the same. He laughed, said Locke was a common enough name in the Midlands. But I can't stop thinking about it. What if they're related? William could be working with Becky to bring me down. I know they were both adopted. What if they got adopted by the same people? My god, Lucy, do you know what kind of trouble I would be in if that was true. You've got to help me."

The pieces clicked in my head, but it felt fragile, like a house of cards. "The same surname… You think Becky's his sister?"

"It's a long shot," he admitted, his voice faltering. "But it's something. And I need you to do something else for me as well."

I groaned. "What?"

"I need the fingerprint test rerun. It could change everything."

A pain shot across my brow, tension building between my eyes. "Didn't William already do that?"

"That's the point, Lucy," he said, his voice hardening. "I don't trust him. Please… you have to do this. If at the end of it all you still think I'm guilty I promise to leave you alone."

My heart raced. Joe's calm resolve sent a chill down my spine. "Alright," I agreed. "I'll get on it."

"Thank you. I love you."

I swallowed hard, tears burning my eyes. "Me too." And I did, so very much, more than I thought I could bear. I desperately wanted him to be innocent.

"I'll call you tomorrow, three o'clock. Can you do that?"

I nodded though he couldn't see me. "Yes."

The line went dead, and I slumped back, my mind reeling.

*****

The next day, the phone buzzed in my hand. I answered, knowing it was Joe.

"Hi Lucy." His voice came out in a rush, revealing his frayed nerves. "Any news?"

I exhaled slowly, trying to keep my voice steady. "Yes and no. Sid's already working on it. The police are rechecking the fingerprints, but we'll need a statement from William. A receipt, confirmation—anything that ties Becky to that burner phone. And don't tip him off, Joe. You've got to be careful."

He sighed in relief. "I'll ask, but Lucy, what about the link between Becky and William?"

I chewed my lip, frustrated that I couldn't wave a wand and make everything alright. "It'll take longer. Did William grow up in the Midlands?"

"Solihull, I think."

"That's something. Becky lived around there too. I'm going through social media profiles, contacting anyone I can find who might know them. Dad's reaching out to a friend to check the rotas—making sure Becky doesn't catch wind of this."

Joe's breath hitched. "Lucy, William's pushing for a plea deal. Tomorrow... says I'll get a lighter sentence."

A rush of certainly hit me. "You can't trust him. Joe, get another lawyer."

"It's too late. He's putting the pressure on."

"Joe, listen to me. It's not over. We still have time."

He let out a nervous laugh. "Thanks for the suit. For tomorrow."

I pressed my lips together, fighting the dread that clawed at me. "Tell the truth, Joe. Let us work in the shadows. Don't let him get to you."

His voice cracked. “I love you, Lucy.”

Tears welled up in my eyes again. “I’ll be there tomorrow. Outside the court. I’ll have another lawyer ready, just in case. Joe, you’ve got to be brave. This is our future on the line.”

Silence stretched between us, the horror of events conspired against us and our happiness. All I could hear was Joe’s shallow breathing. There was nothing left to say. I hung up, praying we weren’t too late.

Chapter 18

Joe—Out of Time

I PACED THE SMALL, cold room, my hands trembling, eyes locked on the faint glimmer of daylight filtering through the barred window. It felt distant, taunting, as if freedom itself were slipping away. They were offering me five years. Five years in exchange for everything I've ever known. I turned towards William, my pulse quickening. *Could I really sign away my life for a crime I didn't commit?*

"Joe, I'm telling you, this is the best deal you'll ever get." William kept his voice steady, devoid of emotion, his face displaying as much empathy as a dead fish. "Five years for a plea deal. Behave yourself, and you could be out in two and a half. It's a gift."

His words rattled in my head like broken glass. *I'm innocent.* The truth of that thought echoed through the room, but it rang hollow, meaningless against the mountain of evidence piled up against me.

"Not necessarily, William. I'm not guilty. You know that," I muttered, though the conviction in my voice was already eroding.

"The evidence doesn't care, Joe. It's solid. Without the plea deal, you'll be looking at fifteen years—minimum. By the time you get out, you'll be old, broken. Lucy won't be there, waiting for you. She'll have moved on."

His words landed like a punch. The thought of Lucy, of her moving on, hit harder than any prison sentence. Before I could respond, there was a sharp knock at the door. A policeman stepped inside; his face unreadable.

"Mr William Locke, Mr Joseph Browne, the Crown Court is ready for you. Please follow me."

William didn't bother looking up as he gathered his papers, his calmness a contrast to the rising storm inside me. "Joe," he said quietly, "hold your head up high. It's five years or fifteen. You know what to do."

The walk along the corridor and up the spiral staircase to the courtroom was like marching toward my own execution. With each step, dread coiled tighter around my throat. The grandeur of the Crown Court crashed over me like a tidal wave the moment we stepped inside.

The air was heavy with the scent of polished wood and lingering dust, while the soaring ceilings echoed the hushed whispers of spectators. Its towering, dark-panelled walls seemed to close in, adorned with intricate carvings and historical portraits that stared down with judgment. The atmosphere was thick with history, the solemnity of justice, and an almost tangible fear. The presence of countless verdicts passed in this place hung in the air, nearly suffocated me.

We sat waiting, my mind whirling, unable to settle. My skin prickled with nerves. *What if this all goes wrong? What if this is it?*

A voice announced from the doorway. "Mr Joseph Browne, Court Six is ready for you now."

I stood, my legs shaky beneath me, nausea rising in waves. This was it. I cast a glance at William. His expression remained flat, cold.

"Remember, Joe, this is a serious crime. Take the deal."

Taking a deep breath I entered the courtroom. The pulse in my temples throbbed, thoughts spiralling as I climbed the steps. Life without Lucy... the wretchedness of having a record... a future that might never happen.

"All rise," the bailiff announced as the judge entered the room, a figure of authority that sent a chill down my spine.

I stood, trying to steady my breath.

The judge's gaze fell upon me, and the room seemed to shrink. He gave a short incline of the head at the Recorder, who stood up.

The Recorder's voice boomed, "Can the defendant indicate at this stage if he intends to plead guilty or not guilty?"

William had made it clear: a guilty plea would offer leniency, a sliver of hope. But the thought of confessing to something I didn't do made my throat tighten. My mind raced back to the moments with Lucy, to the life we'd dreamed of, to a future that now felt like it hung by a thread. I needed her here, now, beside me.

With trembling hands, I stood taller, forcing my voice to rise above the storm inside me.

"Not guilty, Your Honour."

William's expression turned to stone. He shot me a look of thinly veiled disgust, before standing up.

"Your Honour, as this is my client's first offence, and given his strong ties to the community and lack of prior criminal record, I respectfully submit that he poses no flight risk. I ask the court to grant Mr Joseph Browne bail under appropriate conditions."

The judge's cold eyes landed on me once more. "As this is your first offence, I will grant bail until the next trial. The hearing date is to be agreed upon. The conditions of your bail are as follows: You will reside at your home address, confined indoors between the hours of ten and eight. You are to have no contact with Rebecca Locke, nor will you return to The Hedgeway. Technology use is restricted, and you will report to the police station weekly. A sum of ten thousand pounds will be required, which will be forfeited should you fail to attend. Any breach of these conditions, and you will be remanded in custody. Do you understand?"

I nodded, my vision blurring at the edges. It felt like I was floating, the words heavy but distant, muffled by the pounding in my ears.

Nodding, with my vision blurred at the edges, I had the sensation of floating. The judge's words boomed heavy like a gong, and yet distant, muffled by the pounding in my ears.

Outside the courtroom, William cast me a withered glare. "I can't represent you anymore, Joe. The evidence is overwhelming. You've been a fool not to listen."

The floor tilted beneath me.

"I'll find a new lawyer," I managed, the words slipping out through the fog in my head. "I'll need the files, receipts, everything you've gathered. Send me your invoice."

William gave a curt nod, already walking away, his back turned as he headed to the nearby coffee shop where, I knew, Becky would be waiting for him.

Thirty minutes later, Lucy and I were driving home. Free for now, but for how long?

Out on Bail

Driving into the garage felt like a surreal victory, though I couldn't shake the lingering uncertainty. We ate a quiet lunch, then walked through the streets in a daze, clinging to a fragile sense of normality. The silence of the world outside pressed in, and I couldn't help but think of how much everything had changed.

"Mum and Dad are coming round with Sid tonight. Is that okay?" Lucy asked, her voice a little too bright.

I forced a smile. "Of course. I hope they believe me now. I still remember the way your parents looked at me at the airport... like I was already guilty."

She nodded. "Dad's come around. Mum... well, she always follows him. They're trying to protect me."

Later that day, they arrived, bringing with them a heavy air of expectations and unspoken judgments. Patrick, ever the practical one, wasted no time.

"Joe, Carl Newman has agreed to represent you; he comes with the highest recommendations and it's said he's the best you can find in criminal law. He's already requested the evidence from William Locke, and the burner phone is with the police, but Carl's arranged to have it tested tomorrow."

I blinked back tears, their kindness almost unbearable. "Thank you, Patrick, Nancy. I don't know how I'll ever repay you. I've been so stupid calling William, somehow having the same surname felt like a stupid coincidence, I never thought for a moment they were related."

Patrick shook his head. "Forget it, son. You got yourself out of that mess. Now let's keep you out of jail."

Lucy squeezed my hand. "That's the dream, right?"

I nodded, with tears welling up. Patrick had called me 'son,' and in that moment, the dam inside me broke. I crumpled, sobbing as all the fear, guilt, and relief flooded out. Lucy held me close, and I let myself fall apart.

Sid cleared his throat, pulling out papers and a flip chart like we were in a business meeting. "I've been digging. William and Becky are adopted siblings. They haven't seen each other in years, but their family is still connected. Becky has been setting you up for a while, Joe."

My head snapped up; eyes wide. "What?"

Sid nodded, flipping through his notes. "William left you and drove straight to Becky' we have him arriving on CCTV. We think as soon as you mentioned her full name, he knew who she was. And the burner phone was purchased before you took the job at the Hedgeway."

The room spun, pieces of the puzzle falling into place. "I... I didn't realize. She really set me up...?"

Sid grinned. "We're getting closer, mate. The phone is still an issue, but we're on it."

Lucy raised her glass, her smile full of defiance. "To Joe, my soul mate. We'll get you through this."

The weight of their support crashed into me again, and I broke. "I don't deserve any of you."

Nancy smiled softly. "Come on, Joe. Start believing in yourself."

Weeks Later

For a moment, I allowed myself to dream. But the gossip and stares whenever Lucy and I ventured out shattered that illusion. Friends turned their backs, and all I had was time. Endless time to replay every moment, every mistake. My life, even if I walked free, would never be the same.

Lucy's optimism was a light I couldn't reach. "When this is over, we're going back to Puerto Pollensa. We'll start trying for a baby."

All I managed was a faint smile, uncertainty creeping in and tightening around me. I wanted to reassure her, but the hollow ache inside told me there was nothing left to cling to.

"Let's hope we get that far."

Judgement Day

The oppressive atmosphere of the courtroom closed in around me as I took my seat in the dock. My heart raced as Becky took the witness stand, her eyes flashing with a mixture of anger and smug satisfaction. A plain black dress hugged her body replacing her normal colourful attire. With her hair pinned in a bun, she didn't look like the woman I knew. The Crown's Barrister treated her like a victim, painting me as the monster.

Carl waited until it was his turn to cross-examine. His tone was sharp, focused. "Miss Locke, who purchased the burner phone?"

Becky's eyes locked on mine, venomous. "Joe. He must have, how else did the children get the messages?"

Carl's expression didn't waver. "And the receipt? Do you have it?"

Becky faltered. "No. But he probably does."

"Miss Locke, are you aware that all mobile phones have unique identifiers? Things like an IMEI number, which is permanently linked to the device?"

Becky's brow furrowed. "I… I guess so."

"Do you also know that phone companies track the activation of each device? They record the first time the phone connects to their network, including the date and the location of that activation."

A flicker of uncertainty crossed Becky's face, her eyes darting around the room. "I didn't know that."

"Well, they do. And I've looked into the records for the phone in question. According to the service provider, that phone wasn't first activated by my client. It was activated in a completely different location, long before he even had access to it." Carl paused, letting his words sink in. "Would you care to guess whose name is listed as the purchaser of that phone?"

Becky shifted uncomfortably. "I don't know…"

"The name on the account is Rebecca Locke. You," Carl said, leaning in slightly, his voice cold. "The phone was purchased by you, activated by you, and used by you long before my client ever saw it."

Becky swallowed. The courtroom was silent, tension hanging in the air.

"So tell me, Miss Locke," Carl continued, his voice cutting through the silence, "are you still sure my client is the one who used this phone? Or do you have something else to confess?"

Becky's gaze flickered, her lips twitching into a smile that didn't reach her eyes. Her fragility, always teetering on the edge of sanity, cracked in front of everyone. She wanted them to know. Her brother, William, sitting in the public gallery, caught the tell-tale sign—the glint of triumph in her eyes, the one he knew all too well. His heart sank. She was about to unravel, to spill everything.

William shot to his feet, panic in his voice. "Don't answer that! Remain quiet, do you hear me? Just shut up, Becky!" His voice grew louder, more frantic, his usual calm replaced by raw fear.

The judge's gavel crashed down. "Sir, you are in contempt of court. Bailiff, take him away."

William's words fuelled something inside Becky. Her fragile composure cracked wide open, and the truth hovered on the edge of her lips, begging to be unleashed.

She hesitated; eyes wide as Carl pressed on. "Answer the question, Miss Locke. Did you frame Mr Browne?"

Her voice screeched. "Of course I did. He wouldn't have had the guts to do it himself. That loser."

The court fell silent. My admiration soared as I watched Carl's unflinching gaze. The Platt's had been right, this man was amazing.

The truth hung in the air like a knife, sharp and cutting. I held my breath. The magnitude of her confession cut through the room like a blade, leaving everything still.

The judge's expression remained impassive, but his movements were deliberate as he rose from the bench. "Counsel, chambers. Now." His voice carried a quiet authority.

Minutes passed, stretching endlessly as the murmurs of the crowd faded. When the police representative was called in, the tension in the room grew thicker, like a storm gathering.

After what felt like an eternity, the doors to the chambers opened, and everyone fell silent once more, waiting.

The Public Verdict

"All rise."

The judge returned; his face impassive as he delivered the words I'd been waiting for.

"The prosecution has confirmed there is insufficient evidence to convict Mr Joseph Browne. I find the defendant not guilty. You are free to leave."

The room blurred as I stumbled out, the enormity of it all crashing down on me. I could barely breathe or comprehend what had happened. I was free.

Lucy's arms wrapped around me, and I clung to her like a lifeline, my heart racing with relief and disbelief. The future open before us, fragile but real.

She smiled up at me, her eyes full of hope. "Now, Joe, let's get on with the rest of our lives. Puerto Pollensa and babies, remember?"

Taking her in my arms, I drew her to me and kissed her, allowing the warmth of her love and strength to pull me back from the edge. "As long as I have you, we can do anything."

And in that moment, I knew we could.

As the courtroom doors closed behind Joe, the stress of false accusations lifted from his shoulders. With a broad smile, a spring in his step, and hope for the future, he raced into the rest of his life as a man reborn. But a dark, heavy shadow now shrouded his life—one he remained blissfully unaware of.

Freedom, yes—he had that. But each passing day would illuminate a little more of the creeping presence that surrounded him, tugging at the edges of his new life. Eyes unseen would track his every move, waiting for him to slip.

Lucy's smile—warm, devoted—masked something deeper. Beneath her fragile exterior were layers he hadn't yet uncovered, hints of struggle, of a mind stretched to the edge. But inside her burned a core of survival, forged from generations of those who faced darkness and emerged stronger, if not unscathed.

Patrick, once a beacon of support, would now watch him with a hawk's intensity, his gaze a silent warning that trust had its limits. Nancy, the doting mother-in-law, would reveal moments of chilling calculation, her words sharp and too deliberate.

Joe had been cleared of a heinous crime, but unknowingly, he had stepped into something far more sinister. The Platts weren't just protective—they were dangerous. Whispers trailed behind him, fragments of conversations just beyond his reach, the burden of secrets buried deep in their shared smiles. And a trail of missing people… from fathers to construction owners and ex-boyfriends. Each day would become a test. One misstep, one wrong question, and the façade would crack.

The danger was no longer a trial. He hadn't just married into a family; he had entered a legacy steeped in blood. And they were watching. Always watching.

And the love of his life, Lucy—so many layers remained hidden. Joe had yet to understand the depths she would sink to survive. If she could endure the shadows of her past, what lengths would she go to protect her future? The answer would chill him to the bone.

Thank you for reading my story, I hope you enjoyed it. If you have a moment to leave me a review on Amazon or Goodreads I would appreciate it.

Thanks again.

JG

Author's Note:

Your well-being matters.

If you have been affected by any of the topics covered in this story, such as bulimia, self-harming, or domestic abuse, please know that you are not alone. Help is available. For support, you can reach out to the following organizations:

UK

Helpline for Eating Disorders

Beat: 0808 801 0677 (for adults) or 0808 801 0711 (for children and young people)

Website: www.beateatingdisorders.org.uk

Helpline for Self-Harm

Samaritans: 116 123 (available 24/7)

Website: www.samaritans.org

Domestic Abuse Helpline

National Domestic Violence Helpline: 0808 2000 247 (available 24/7)

Website: www.nationaldahelpline.org.uk

US

Helpline for Eating Disorders

National Eating Disorders Association (NEDA): 1-800-931-2237

Website: www.nationaleatingdisorders.org

Helpline for Self-Harm

National Suicide Prevention Lifeline: 1-800-273-TALK (1-800-273-8255) (available 24/7)

Website: www.suicidepreventionlifeline.org

Domestic Abuse Helpline

National Domestic Violence Hotline: 1-800-799-SAFE (1-800-799-7233) (available 24/7)

Website: www.thehotline.org

Printed in Great Britain
by Amazon

49543826R00119